NEW JERICHO

B.B. Allen

Fulton Books
Meadville, PA

Published by Fulton Books 2022

Illustrations created by Michael Hines

ISBN 979-8-88505-252-8 (paperback)
ISBN 979-8-88505-253-5 (digital)

Printed in the United States of America

CHAPTER 1

Trying to Be Normal

Underneath the pouring rain, a father held an umbrella over two boys—one thirteen years and the other just five—who were standing in front of a casket while the priest gave a sermon. The older boy was crying, but the younger held a stone-cold face as the other held his hand.

Eight years had passed since that day...

Inside a medium-sized bedroom, a moaning woman was on top of a man in his bed, having sex, while the other sat on his face. They took turns sniffing cocaine, enjoying the time with some music in the background.

Suddenly, a bang from the bedroom door hit the wall as a man came through it!

The women screamed as he grabbed the bag of drugs sitting on a small table not far from the bed. He quickly looked for an exit, noticed an open window, and jumped out.

The man who was being pleasured, Royce, jumped up, shoving both of the women off, gesturing the other to stop with his hands to grab his boxers.

"I'm going to fuck you up!" Royce yelled, trying to get dressed.

Royce, with unexpected speed, jumped through the window after him, but the stranger was now a few feet ahead. They both reached a random backyard and jumped over five- to six-foot fences with prestigious ease across each one. The man kept periodically looking back, surprised by Royce's speed and strength.

The chase continued.

They finally reached a ten-story apartment building. And in between each wall from one complex to the next, the man was climbing, finally reaching the roof where he disappears from Royce's sight. Royce ran up the stairs in a crisscross motion every fifth to sixth step, finally reaching the top floor. He yanked on to a ledge, pulling his body weight up to the roof.

The man stood there, looking pale but without a shortness of breath. Royce didn't flinch at the man who was frozen, staring at him, just waiting.

"Give me the drugs back, and I will let you walk away with just a limp!" Royce threatened. The man sized up Royce and saw a six-foot-one tall, toned Black man with short wavy hair.

"You are fast and strong for a normal, but I'm gonna beat you within an inch of your life and then make you one of us," the man responded with no fear.

Royce clenched his fist and charged head-on when the man simultaneously did the same. Royce was able to blast the first two punches, but the man dodged them as if they were in slow motion.

He then managed to get close to his opponent's face, but the attacker caught his fist and threw him back. This pushed him on a small shed that cracked into pieces in the shape of Royce's back.

Royce quickly got up, not fazed, and threw a roundhouse kick toward his face, but again, the man caught his leg and pushed him through satellite dishes that broke in half. Royce wasn't hurt. He got back up again, not fazed. His energy was something he could measure, and he knew he still had plenty of it.

The attacker threw the first punch at the standoff. But Royce was able to dodge a couple of them before he got a hard hit, which was a three-punch combo thrown at him from his left side, which made him fall. The attacker stood over him, smiling, but Royce used this to his advantage and punched him in the stomach unexpectedly with a strike to the rib. The man let out a grunt and folded over to his side. Royce then headbutted him under his chin, which caused a piece of his tongue to start bleeding from the edges of his teeth. The red liquid started gushing out on the right side and down his face as he fell backward. The sound from the drop was rough but still didn't override his yell.

Royce bent over to grab his shirt, pulling him close in with one last punch to the face, causing a mini shockwave that vibrated through the air. This threw his opponent across other satellites that were lined up on the edge, leaning on the opposite side, breaking each one. Royce walked slowly toward him when he noticed his teeth on the ground. They were elongated, making him realize what he was.

Royce smiled.

"I hit hard, don't I?" Royce stated with cockiness.

The man started to laugh as if he felt no pain, which made Royce angry. He grabbed him again to slam him down on the edge of the building, causing it to break the brick and mortar around him. But they both fell, bouncing off a fire escape, crashing loudly against the side of the building.

Royce grabbed on to anything he could, but the attacker's head got caught on the side of the metal between a railing and the fire escape. He tried to grab him swiftly, gripping the side of him, but it caused his head to clip off as they hit the ground.

Royce landed on his back as the attacker fell to the other side of him.

"I guess that was too much," Royce said with his head lifted, trying to look up at the scene, but it only lasted a second before he passed out.

*****

You could hear a slur of muffled voices.

As Royce opened his eyes, his blurred vision finally became clearer. Three men were standing in front of him.

"Hello, Royce, my name is Ward, and this is Van. We are here from the NJPD," Ward said while leaning over him about fifteen inches away.

"Mr. Ward, I would like for him to rest more before you question him." A man in a doctor's suit with a clipboard spoke from behind, who obviously directed them to the room.

"You can leave," Van demanded rudely. The doctor didn't respond but gave a disappointing look as he walked out.

"We know who you are and what you've been up to. And we really can't decide what to do with you yet," Ward indicated with a condescending tone.

"First of all, you don't know me. *And* I haven't done anything," Royce responded, confused and exhausted as he tried to move.

"Hi, I'm Van, nice to meet you. How about murder?" Van asked without pausing from his first sentence.

"Van, is it?" Royce asked sarcastically, ignoring his question.

"Yes. Answer the fucking question," Van attacked.

Ward put his hand out, gesturing to calm down. But Van didn't take his eyes off Royce.

"Well then, fuck you and this other guy because we all know that was a vamp. So what does it fucking matter?" Royce stated while slowly closing his eyes. He wanted to sleep, but it didn't look like they were leaving.

With no hesitation, Ward decided to try another threat.

"Then we can use the drugs and guns we found at your place now, can't we?"

Royce stayed silent, not knowing what else to defend himself with. A minute then passed, and they all realized the meeting was over.

Ward handed Royce his card.

"When you get out of here, stop by the precinct and we'll talk," Ward encouraged. They proceeded to turn and walk out. Van followed Ward.

"See you later, Royce." Van smiled with sarcasm, not looking back.

Royce took a deep sigh. His mind was trying to figure out how they knew what he was up to. He started to look for his remote. The breaking news was on.

"Allegedly, today a vamp was killed by a normal," the reporter said with anxiety and excitement.

A scene with a crowd was everywhere on the screen.

Royce let out an angry sigh when Ward appeared on the screen, giving an interview as he stood close next to the reporter.

"Are the rumors true, Mr. Ward?"

"Well, after eight years, we found the mayor's son, and yes, he can kill a vamp with his bare hands, so we are still in question about it all."

Ward looked restless speaking into the microphone with his hands on his hips. However, he continued.

"But we ask that you let him rest and respect his privacy. We'll have more up-to-date news later."

The reporter nodded her head yes, but she had one last question. "Are the vamps' nest any closer to being found?"

"No, but the leader was killed, so looking for the nest next might be easier. And just remember, even though it is illegal to be a vamp, don't try to kill them. Leave it to us. We don't need any more people turning."

The reporter looked like she wanted to ask something else as she whisked the mic back to her, but Ward nodded his head to say, "I'm not taking any more questions, thank you."

Royce took another deep sigh and then looked down at his abrasions, wondering when he was getting out as the weather report followed.

*****

They finally released Royce after two days. When he arrived home, he looked around, making sure everything was in its place. It wasn't much to look at, but he always knew where his shit was.

He was glad to be home but also didn't want to be there. The hospital kept him one day too long. He showered, shaved, and got dressed. Once he made sure his wounds were wrapped up right underneath his clothes, he entered the garage. He snapped on the light, moving the cover that was over it, uncovering a hidden button. When pushed, the floor opened up with two doors sliding horizontally. A sharp and shiny red truck with chromed wheels rose up. It made a *zip-zip* noise as the tires rotated.

Royce smiled as he walked toward it.

He used his thumb to imprint on the truck door panel, allowing it to slowly open. He sighed with relief as he sat on his white leather seats to put it in gear.

*****

The entrance to the club was bumping. It was loud with a handsome crowd. The door guy was checking people in while others waited in line. But Royce knew the club owners, and he didn't have to wait.

"Hey, Royce, how's it going, my man?" The bouncer shook his hand with a slight hug, immediately turning to open the door for him.

Royce went straight to the bar. He ordered a drink, and two girls immediately rushed over. "Hey, cutie, you're Royce from the news, right?" the first girl in the short black dress asked. Royce stared at her muscular legs, almost forgetting to answer the question.

"Well?" The second girl grabbed his arm, poking him for attention.

"Yeah," Royce answered when he turned to look at the other girl's breast.

"He's even sexier in person," the girl in the black dress said, smiling and grabbing his other arm.

"So did you really kill the vamp with your hands?" the second asked while flaunting her breast.

"Yes," Royce answered while putting his drink down. "But we will talk about it more at my house, shall we?" Royce put his arms around the girls to give a nudge. As they smiled to press forward toward the exit, the glasses behind the bar exploded! They ducked simultaneously, and people started screaming and running.

"Follow me!" Royce signaled the girls, heading toward an exit, then running to the truck. They hopped in his red Avalanche as another explosion went off behind them.

"Why were they bombing?" she asked while fixing her hair and the straps on her black dress.

"I have no idea. But if it was vamps, they normally don't attack crowds in a club," Royce responded, but deep down he knew something was odd about it.

Royce showed the girls in. They immediately looked around the place, thinking he would have something nicer but only smiled as he handed them a drink.

"So what do you women have in mind?" he asked, sitting in between them.

The girl in the black dress started to remove Royce's belt. The other one chugged her drink and then started kissing his neck. They both slowly moved lower and lower, going down on him, taking turns. His erection was strong and hard when he laid his head against the back head of the couch. He started to drift and heard noises but didn't know if he was dreaming. It sounded like a man yelling. The girls stopped to look up. They could hear it too.

"Hello, Royce, die for me!" an echo came from outside.

"Who the FUCK?" Royce opened his eyes quickly. The girls tried to scatter when seconds later, a hail of gunfire traveled through the house. Royce dove to the floor when he saw both women slaughtered by the mass shooting, becoming body shields unexpectedly, and the blood spread everywhere.

Red light beams infested the living room. Royce started to count them in his mind as he articulated a plan to move his body quickly underneath something before the next attack. The gunfire went off again, so he pushed the fridge out of the way by his feet to get behind it, waiting for it to stop. He wanted to rush over the counter to open a secret box hidden underneath his island, where his guns were, but he couldn't see. Red and white flashes of light were bombing the entire room at different angles. The gunfire stopped as voices were being thrown around him.

Royce tried to peek out and squinted against the bright lights, trying to see or hear something. A man's shadow was standing there over three dead bodies, and the holes in the walls were revealing a few more.

"Hey, Royce, can I get a ride to the precinct? I had to run over here," a sarcastic request from Van sounded out loud with no tension in his voice.

Royce squinted his eyes.

"How the hell did you do that? Wait, who are you?" Royce started to question, not realizing who it was or what just happened.

"I'm Van. We met the other day."

After the shock wore off, Royce stood up to look for his keys.

They finally walked over to the garage from the only door left standing. When Royce opened it, he regretted not lowering his truck into the secret compartment. It was covered in bullet holes.

"Fuck! Look at my truck!" Royce whimpered. Royce leaned over to hug his Avalanche with one tear. "Look at my baby. I'm so sorry, I'm so sorry."

Van stared, looking extremely confused.

"Uh, can we go now?" Van asked underneath his breath. Royce stared at him and, with a sarcastic gesture, told him to get in.

*****

The precinct was busy and chaotic as usual. Royce was still venting about his truck, and Van was nodding his head as they walked in, demonstrating an I-don't-care look with nods as Royce looked to him for sympathy.

"Royce, shut up," Van finally said in a soft tone when he opened the door to Ward's office. Royce stopped in his tracks, wanting to punch Van in the face.

"Well, try to fix it, okay?" Van pointed for Royce to keep walking.

"No, I don't want anybody to touch her. Fuck you," Royce responded as he walked in.

"Whatever, bro." Van shut the door behind them.

"It's too bad you didn't come sooner. Seventeen people didn't have to die, you know?" Ward showed him the closest chair with sarcasm.

"That's not my fucken fault. Wait, what, seventeen?" Royce asked with confusion, noticeably from his eyebrows.

"The people at the club, the women you fucked, the ones Van killed saving you," Ward explained.

"The people at the club ain't my fault, and a vamp shouldn't count," Royce answered sarcastically.

"Oh, come on, you know humans work for vamps, and the bombs at the club were for you," Ward said, leaning up toward his desk to show seriousness.

Royce stayed quiet, trying to register what he just said.

"Listen, you killed a vamp. The only people I know that can do that are the ones that work here." Ward changed the subject but indirectly made a statement.

"So you're offering me a job?" Royce asked sarcastically.

"Yes, in our special unit," Ward confirmed.

Royce rolled his eyes because he was kidding.

"You've got to be kidding me? I don't need a damn job from some damn moron running it." Royce became angry, knowing they were trying to sucker him into it.

"Listen. For one, I want you to explain to me how you're going to leave this place? Because no one on the street trusts you anymore. Why do you think there were two attempts on your life last night? People want you dead. The only protection you're going to have now is us because eventually, it's not going to be the one-on-one battles you've had if you go out there alone."

After Ward made his speech to him, he threw a newspaper at Royce. "Read this."

Royce's eyes glanced over, impeding some anger.

"Are you fucking serious? You had an article published that said that I took a permanent job here? What the fuck is wrong with you?" Royce asked with animosity in his throat.

Royce paused to think.

"Those hits were because of you?" Royce stood up to push his chair back with his right foot.

"You will always be marked man in the streets, but I will make sure that ends with us," Ward confirmed his manipulation.

"You guys are some fucking assholes," Royce said, shaking his head. "But whatever."

"I knew your answer before you did. I'm an empath and a tactician. I'm captain of the special unit for a reason, and I did this for a reason, not just to save your ass but to help something bigger than you, Royce," Ward explained with a condescending tone.

Outside of the precinct, there was a press conference being held. Ward waited to drop the news until Royce agreed. He signaled him to walk outside. He needed him to confirm the legitimacy of his claims. Royce was mad, but what could he do? He was being instructed by *his boss* now.

It was loud and crowded behind the precinct with cops guarding the crowd. Royce ignored most of it when he saw a figure standing on a rooftop a couple of blocks away. Ward was going on and on about how it was great to have Royce join the team in the background through the PA system, but Royce was trying to zoom in on the roof with his eyes to see who it was. Ward grabbed him by the shoulder as if they were pals, breaking his concentration. He moved away from Ward to get comfortable over the mic to answer some questions. He tried to take one last peek at the roof, but the figure was gone.

"Training starts tomorrow." Ward grabbed the mic back. The conference ended even though many were shouting out last-minute questions.

Ward, Van, a couple of cops, and Royce all turned to walk back inside.

Ward touched Royce to say, walking side by side, "Listen, don't think you are that special. We always announce our detectives."

Royce didn't feel like having a conversation with Ward's sarcasm.

"I'm going to head home. I'll grab my things and meet you back at the precinct later," Royce said, barely looking at Ward, walking out.

"Bye, Royce, good to see you again!" Van said to get one last smirk of sarcasm out, waving him off.

CHAPTER 2

The Mayor

When Royce arrived at his home, there were a couple of black SUVs parked in different sections on the street, including his driveway. He walked past them and stared but didn't ask questions. He finally entered his house when he saw a man looking around in a black suit, staring at his destroyed property.

"Hello, Royce, long time no see." The six-foot-two-tall man with yellowish eyes, salt-and-pepper hair, in a black suit, red button up, black tie, and black dress shoes said as he grabbed his collar to straighten his coat.

"What did I do to get a visit from the mayor?" Royce asked.

"I'm not here as your mayor. I'm here as your father. My son is back. It wouldn't be fatherly like if it didn't come say hello now, would it? And (with a sigh) I must say, this is a nice shithole you have here," William finished with sarcasm.

"William, what the fuck do you want?" Royce demanded, refusing to acknowledge him as his father.

"I came here to give you a penthouse downtown. You'll be more comfortable, plus it will make me look good," his father responded back with the same tone.

"I don't want shit from you. Now get out of here before I beat the fuck out of you!" Royce demanded as he stared straight-faced.

"I'd like to see you try it, son," William responded as he stared back with no movement.

Royce almost contemplated for a second, but then rushed to his father with anger. William threw a quick jab which hit Royce in the face, making him stumble backward.

"I see you still need to be the first one to attack," William said with a condescending tone, but Royce stood back up in a flash to repeat the attack. William stopped him with a blow to his face, quickly connecting combination punches. Royce fumbled from the right to the left several times before falling. He kicked up, trying to land his foot on his father's face but missed.

"You're still too slow, son. You have been fighting with normals for eight years, and it has made you weak," William explained in a fatherly tone.

Royce started fist fighting again, not wanting to give up, sending a shock wave through the house. William blocked each one like eating a piece of cake. Being caught by his father's hand pushed Royce back to the ground. The last punch Royce made wasted his last breath.

"So you want to use your powers?" William asked in a fatherly tone.

William grabbed Royce by his shirt, forcing him to stand up. He hit him so hard that this shockwave actually made a visible sound wave. He then threw an uppercut to the chin, almost lifting Royce to the ceiling and then making him fall hard to the floor.

Royce was done and out of breath.

William didn't move from his position. He stared at Royce while fixing his tie to turn and leave.

But before he left, he decided he has something left to say. "We will fix up this place tomorrow, and I hope you take me up on my offer soon."

Royce stayed silent.

Van walked up right when William was leaving. They stared at each other down as they passed. "Nice to see you, Mr. Mayor," Van sarcastically said with a smirk.

"Get my son some help," William suggested as he kept walking with no eye contact. Van immediately helped Royce up to help him reach the destroyed couch.

"Why would your father do you like this?" Van asked with confusion and curiosity. Royce looked at Van and then made a sigh, obviously not meaning to answer.

"Well, if it helps, we got your truck fixed, and everything else is done," Van said as he patted Royce on the leg like long-time buddies.

"What the fuck do you want?" Royce's ego kicked in with anger, holding on to the pain in his leg.

"Don't be mad at me because your dad kicked your ass. I'm just trying to help," Van said as he sat down with his legs crossed.

"Anyways, it is time to go to work! We need you to talk to this guy," Van said with excitement in his eyes.

"I think I need a little time to myself," Royce responded.

"I bet you do," Van responded in an uncaring voice.

Royce realized that he had no choice in the matter, and with a deep sigh, he did his best to stand up straight and put on his coat.

*****

The club is called Philiverse. It was outside the city limits. The area looks apocalyptic as it stands within the ruins. The club was obviously freshly built, as it was the only thing on the street that looked new.

An eight-foot grunge guy with a huge sledgehammer head was guarding the door. His smile was creepy, but he greeted everyone with it. He had an anvil tattoo on his chest that complimented his scariness.

"Hello, Tank! How have you been?" Van said to him as if they were best friends.

Tank stayed silent as his smile disappeared. He was keeping an eye out at all angles of the entrance. There was a group of hot chicks in line, but Royce and Van didn't mind walking in front of them to get closer to Tank.

"We're here to see your boss," Van demanded, pulling a toothpick out of his teeth, throwing it to the floor near Tank's foot.

Tank kept his blank face, looking at Van as if he was about to get punched in it.

"Can we get in or not?" Royce sounded impatient and decided to pick a fight that he probably couldn't deliver on. His dad for sure reduced some of his powers that evening, but he didn't care. He was mad.

Tank stayed staring, so Royce tried to walk past, but Tank put his hand on his shoulder to stop him. Royce looked at his shoulder and then at Tank.

"He's not seeing anybody now," Tank made clear with his grunge direct tone.

"We are NJPD, and we need to talk to him. Take your hand off me," Royce tried to sound important.

Van grabbed Royce and tried to calm him.

"Listen, Tank," Van started to say, but Tank growled with bad breath smoke coming out of his mouth. Van waved it out of his face with a painful squint that drew from the smell.

"Did you hear what I said!" Tank repeated.

"Fuck you, you fucking ogre!" Royce yelled out.

"Royce, calm down. Let me handle this." Van tried to pull him back from Tank's face.

"Nah, I'm fucking tired of people disrespecting us!"

"Royce, the only person giving you shit was your dad. Stop making things worse. I'll handle it from here," Van directed in a bossy tone.

"Fuck you. Fuck him!" Royce pointed his fingers to both, directing the fuck yous accordingly.

The line behind them started to back away slowly.

Tank grabbed and swung his sledgehammer downward, tearing the concrete underneath Royce's legs. But Royce could not dodge it and tried to block with his right arm, breaking his shoulder bone, knocking him back ten feet. He didn't have time to think, and a drop of blood came out from one of the wounds his father already inflicted. Tank then raised his sledgehammer for another blow.

"OKAY, THAT'S ENOUGH. Escort them in, Tank," a voice demanded over the PA system.

The crowd moved back in line as Tank grabbed Royce to help him up and threw him over his shoulder.

"What the hell are you doing? Put me down. Watch my shoulder, asshole," Royce yelled in pain as Van started to giggle.

"Let's go," Tank instructed as he singled the other bouncer to take over the door. Van was still shaking his head at Royce, trying to understand his childlike behavior.

They walked through the club, seeing people drinking, dancing, and live music. They finally reached the second floor where a modern, eccentric office emerged. The floor was made of silver marble, and the walls had large statues piercing on each end in white pearl-like material. The furniture was shiny black leather and looked very expensive.

Tank tossed Royce on the couch as if he was a rag doll. "Sit," Tank said with a smile.

"Damn, man, I said watch my shoulder!" Royce yelled again in pain.

Royce tried to move his arms but couldn't budge and stayed sitting as he saw a man walk in who was five-foot-eleven, a Black man with short hair, dark shades, thick beard, gold chains, salmon-colored dress shirt, skull belt buckle, black leather pants, and dress shoes.

"Who the hell is this guy?" Royce said in amazement at the man's outfit.

"Hey, Philario, it's been a while," Van said, still standing.

Tank turned to listen and drew closer to Van. Van then did a fake karate move when Tanks walked by to walk out. The stare was intense, but Van didn't move his position.

"Yes, it has. So what can I do to help the NJPD? Since you risked your lives coming down here 'n' all," Philario said as he sat upright, closing his hand with crossed fingers.

"Oh, you know who the fuck we are?" Royce stood up, trying to get his manhood back.

"We don't risk our lives to do anything," he continued when Van took a deep stare, confused why Royce doesn't get a clue.

"Hey, kid, you must not realize where you are? You're not in the city. NJPD has no jurisdiction here or protection. I would be careful if I were you," Philario reacted calmly.

"Whatever, man." Royce thought about it and sat back down. Van shook his head in disapproval and turned back to Philario.

"A week ago, someone put a hit on Royce. Can you tell me who it was? Many lives are being lost for this guy, and we want to know why," Van asked, sitting, now facing Philario.

"You need a favor, and I need a favor." Philario agreed to talk. "There are some armored trucks that drive by and shoot at my club. Tank is way too slow to catch them," he continued.

"Okay, say no more. I'll take care of it. But you're going to have to turn your jammer off," Van instructed as he looked around the room.

Philario pushed a button under his desk. Red lights began to flash outside of the window and in the hall. A low siren started to play. Van pulled up his sleeve and clicked a button on a device on his forearm. A holoscreen appeared in front of his eyes. It showed a bird's-eye view of the area, and he could make it travel to different sections as he directed it with his mind and fingers. He pinpointed the trucks in the area. He moved a satellite to target it. A laser zoned in on the trucks, and within seconds, they blew up simultaneously. The holoscreen closed.

"DONE. Now tell me what we need to know," Van demanded.

"Well, I heard it was the mayor," Philario said with a smile.

"Heard or know?" Van questioned.

"That's right, Royce, your dad. Or father, or William. Whatever you call him these days." He looked at Royce with sarcasm in his eyes.

Royce didn't let it faze him. He hid the emotion with a deep breath that no one could hear. "As far as I know, he doesn't want me dead. But whatever, man." Royce didn't believe him.

"He wants to test your skill level. You had to fight back, didn't you? I'm sure he could use you on his team. We all know that you have superhuman abilities. You've become a weapon. Or they may need to eliminate you. Who knows," Philario said with a careless tone.

"Thanks," Van said when he turned to Royce.

Van singled Royce to get up and move out. As they walked out, Tank walked in. He turned to close the door as Royce and Van got in the elevator.

"Did you get it?" Philario asked Tank.

"Yes, sir, some of Royce's blood. Easy to get," Tank smirked.

Philario jiggled the vial that Tank handed him.

*****

"What was that back there?" Royce asked when they hopped in the cop car.

"What?" Van was in a trance, already driving.

"Your arm, the laser, and how did you blow up the truck?"

"Oh, my ability. Well, I'm a normal, if that's what you're wondering," Van said in a childlike voice. "But I'm a master in mixed martial arts. I have genius-level intelligence. So I designed a satellite that lets me find anything I need to find. Me and Gears put it in orbit over the city, and I can control it with the holoscreen on my arm. Mostly cop stuff, nothing personal," Van explained.

"And the truck, how did you blow up the truck?"

"Philario was just testing me. You saw the manpower he has. He's not worried about armored trucks. And he's probably wrong about your dad too."

"Yeah, man, that doesn't make any sense. We don't get along, but he wouldn't take it that far," Royce said but wasn't really sure.

"Yeah, it's obvious from earlier," Van said sarcastically with a giggle.

"Would you shut the fuck up and drive." Royce looked out the window.

Van looked at him but kept driving with a smirk on his face.

*****

Back at the precinct, Ward was sitting at his desk, stroking his forehead, stressed. He could see Van and Royce walking toward him through the glass of his office window, and it made him take a deep breath.

"How's it going, Royce?" Ward asked.

Royce made a face, giving him a silent answer that wasn't pleasant.

"No one said it was going to be a walk in the park." Ward tried to help.

"Man, get on with it," Royce answered without looking directly at him.

"Well, we need you. I will admit that," Ward tried to comfort him in his assholish way.

"It would be nice if you guys would tell me where we're going and why we're going there first," Royce blurted out.

Van leaned forward in his seat. "Yeah, that would be my fault."

Ward ignored the commentary between the two and noticed Royce's bruises and cuts. "Did you get anything?" Ward asked Van.

"Not really. He is saying it's the mayor," Van suggested. Ward nodded and looked at Royce.

"I still need my guns, and it would be nice if I could get the tools I need to work this job." Royce had been wanting to ask.

"The special unit doesn't fight with normals, so you have to find your own weapons that fit you and help you do your job. Now go get healed up, and come back when you're ready to work," Ward stated and told them both to get the fuck out of his office.

CHAPTER 3

It's Radd

For the next few days, Royce stayed home to heal, but the next morning, there was an invitation at the door.

The invitation said,

Come visit sometime, 10067 Dead Street,
Jericho Valley, RADD.

*****

In a rural area, Royce pulled up near a neon sign that was burnt out, somewhat flickering. "What the hell is this?" he said underneath his breath.

A worn-down dark voodoo shop stood in front of him. A five-foot-eleven older Black man with gray eyes and hair, glasses, white short-sleeved, button-up shirt, black khakis with suspenders, and black shoes was standing behind the counter that he could see through the windowpane.

He pulled the glass door open and walked in.

"I was hoping you would come," the old man said.

Royce stayed silent while he stood by the door to look around.

"My name is Radd. I've been watching you on the TV, and I think I can help you."

"Help? How, and with what?" Royce responded with cautiousness.

"You killed a vampire, and I'm sure you know you are special, but you're still a weak link in the NJPD," the old man said in a fatherly tone.

Royce didn't take offense but decided to make something clear. "I haven't even met the rest of the unit, so I really wouldn't know."

"Trust me, Royce, you are. But you don't have to be. You have a really strong bloodline. You just need to be trained," Radd responded while staring at him, hoping he would be receptive.

"Let me guess, you're the perfect man for the job?" Royce responded with sarcasm when he turned back to look into his eyes.

"I'm the only person for the job," Radd confirmed.

"You know nothing about my bloodline, old man. How in the hell are you gonna help me? You look like you could barely lift a finger," Royce insulted him.

"I actually know a lot more than you think, but you have to be willing to let me guide you. You have to trust me, Royce." Radd stayed calm as he encouraged.

"Do you mind if I see these guns on the wall ol' man?" Royce decided to change the subject.

"Good choice. These are matching Rhinos. One light, one dark, and they're very powerful revolvers," he explained as he pulled them down from the wall.

"How much? Royce asked.

"For you, nothing."

"Bullshit," Royce responded with a smirk.

"No bullshit. Just let me give you a tattoo, and they're all yours."

"What? What kind of weird shit are you into ol' man?" Royce backed up and was offended.

"It's not like that, relax. I don't know if you want water, juice, or soda, but while you look around, why don't you grab something?" Radd disappeared to the back of his shop.

Royce turned around and grabbed a water. He was fascinated by another gun on the wall as he finished his bottle of water.

"Let me know if you need anything else!" But right when Royce was going to answer, he started to feel dizzy. He shook his head from left to right, trying to snap out of it, but he suddenly hit the ground and fainted. Radd's voice yelled from the back of the shop.

*****

Royce woke up the next morning in his own bed. He didn't have much memory from the previous day as he got up to wash his face. He realized that his arms and face were finally healed from the fight he had with Tank and his father. He couldn't stop staring at himself in the mirror, fascinated by his healed wounds. He also noticed a heart puzzle tattoo over his heart. He then remembered that he didn't know how it got there or how he got home.

"What the fuck!" Royce yelled and threw the towel to the floor to get dressed. On the top of his table dresser was a note with the Rhinos he saw in ol' man Radd's shop. And there was some shiny gear that looked like hero-type shit for him to wear. The note read,

Enjoy the new gear. It will help absorb some
trauma when you fight.

Royce put on an outfit with black jeans, a blue button up, and a shoulder holster to put the guns in. Last, he put the three-fourth-length leather jacket on from Radd that was tailored to his body.

Royce walked over to the mirror. "Damn! I look good." But he still was going to pay that ol' man another visit.

*****

Royce drove up with bottled-up frustration, but when he walked into his shop, the old man was nowhere to be seen.

"Where are you, old man?"

After a few seconds of silence, Radd came out from behind the curtain. "Hey, back so soon? What can I do for you?" Radd acted as if he didn't know why Royce was visiting.

Royce suddenly grabbed Radd by his shirt to pull him closer, but Radd pulled a knife from his back pocket and cut his hand.

"What the fuck is wrong with you?" Royce said as he clenched his hand closed.

Radd suddenly put his hand across his chest with a tiny bit of force, pushing him across the room where he lands on the couch, becoming perfectly seated.

"You need to relax," Radd calmly said when he walked closer to him.

"Relax! Are you crazy? You tattoo me, and now you just cut me!"

"I'm sure you noticed by now that you heal very quickly. That is how the healing works. But you need to relax in order to heal. So if you relax your hand, you will heal within the next five minutes."

Royce looked shocked, but he couldn't explain how he woke without even a scar. He decided to calm down. When he did, he noticed tingling in his hand and the cut slowly closing.

"See? I told you. Now tell me when you go back to work?" Radd asked if all this was normal.

"I go back in a few days," Royce answered, starting to believe in the ol' man.

"Good. Then your training will start now." Radd put his hand out to shake Royce's newly healed hand.

CHAPTER 4

Four Days

Day 1

Guns were drawn as Van and Ward cased a building to protect themselves from unknown forces. The moonlight seeped through some of the windows in the dark as their shadows slowly cased each step. They were breathing heavily and bleeding, trying to catch their breath.

"What the hell are these things? Do you see any more?" Ward said to Van in a whisper.

"I don't know. The last one damaged the projector on my holo-screen." Van kept messing with it, but nothing was activating.

"Fuck, we are in here blind? We're going to have to get out of here," Ward commanded.

As they were looking for an exit, they heard footsteps and loud screeching. Suddenly, a vampire was running toward them. They both immediately started shooting. The vamp dodged each bullet, jumping from space to space and off the ceiling.

On the last attack from the ground, the vamp reached Ward, which caused him to be thrown down the hall. Ward was trying to stop himself, sliding with his fingernails against the rug, almost losing the grip on his gun.

Van started shooting when the vamp came after him next and grabbed his left arm, but Van kicked him off while shooting him with his right, sending the vamp backward, blowing his face off. Ward was finally able to get up to help, but another vamp suddenly appeared behind him.

"WARD, BEHIND YOU!" Van warned.

Ward immediately turned to start shooting but missed. Van tried to help, but his gun got jammed as Ward walked backward, still shooting everywhere to buy time. Ward clipped off a second red laser handgun and threw it to Van. Van clipped it and shot the vamp in his face right before it bit Ward.

"What the fuck was that? They are stronger and faster." Van looked around, waiting for more, speaking with confusion.

"I don't know," Ward answered with fear too.

They heard more footsteps, and the screeching started to get louder and louder. Van and Ward looked at each other and ran as fast as they could to an exit.

"Where the fuck is backup?" Van was yelling as they were almost out of breath, hauling ass.

They both hit the front doors with their side shoulders, tumbling down the steps, landing two feet away from Buster, a six-foot-five, muscular White man with short red hair and red beard, black full-length leather coat, single-shoulder holster under it, tan button up, black pants, and boots.

He was standing next to his partner, Milo, who was six-foot-four and looked the same but with short blond hair and a gray button up.

"It's about time!" Van yelled at them when they all simultaneously looked at the top of the steps. Four hissing vamps were staring down at them.

Ward and Van got up off the ground, grabbing their guns to aim.

"Be careful, these are not normal vamps," Ward warned. Milo and Buster ignored the comment, ready to rumble!

"Van, let's get out of the way," Ward signaled Van to move quickly.

Buster and Milo charged in, turning into werewolves, as Van and Ward ran to their cop cars. They attacked the first two vamps by biting their heads off, instantly rushing the rest backward, but then the rest of the vamps charged by jumping onto their backs. Buster grabbed ahold of one's necks and pushed him backward, smashing him against the wall behind them. It crushed his body, and he fell to the ground. Buster then took advantage of his standing point and stomped on the vamp's head, crushing it into pieces.

Milo roared as the vamp on his back bit him, but his arm reached back and grabbed the vamp's legs, while his other arm clenched his neck, pulling his head off, tossing it to the ground, splitting the vamp in half. Milo and Buster flex, stretching their neck toward the sky, howling, as they immediately turn back to normal, but they are now both covered in blood.

"I'm glad you are wearing your expanding pants this time," Ward said sarcastically as he waited for them to walk back over.

"I always knew you were jealous of me," Milo responded with a smile as he patted Ward on his back.

"Are you guys okay?" Buster asked Van and Ward.

"Yeah, I think so. What took you guys so long?" Van said with some sarcasm.

"Ward told us not to do anything until you guys came out," Milo answered with confusion.

Ward turned to Van to explain that they needed to trick the vamps to come outside of the building before Milo and Buster could help.

"Are you crazy? Don't do that tactician shit while my life is on the line," Van responded with frustration.

Ward ignored the comment and replied, "Listen, the cleaning crew will be here soon."

Van suddenly realized that Milo was bit. "Hey, are you okay?" Van said when he took a closer look at his neck.

"Yeah, I'm fine. They are a little stronger. Normally, vamp's teeth can't break our skin when we transform, but this one did. Doesn't matter, our metabolism burns through their venom."

Milo gestured to Buster to head out. "We are going to get cleaned up," Milo noted to Van and Ward.

"Report back to NJPD when you can," Ward instructed them as they drove off.

Day 2

A five-foot-five mixed woman with long curly hair, wearing black heels, black jeans, purple shirt, and a black leather duster that glided across the floor. "I hate this. This shit is killing my personal life," Zinda said under her breath as she walked in an abandoned subway with her gun drawn.

Behind her, Angelica, her partner, five feet and seven inches, long sharp nails, short black hair, was wearing black heels, leather pants with a black fitted biker jacket, and had pale skin.

"Well, at least you have a personal life," she tried to joke but then took a whiff in the air. "Wait, I smell something. Shit, they are here," Angelica warned Zinda.

Two vampires walked out from behind a pillar slowly.

"Don't shoot, Zinda. Maybe we can talk," Angelica instructed.

"Are you fucking serious?" Zinda recanted.

"They haven't attacked as soon as they saw us. Let's find out why," Angelica said as she whispered behind her gun.

"Well, don't drop your guard," Zinda warned, not buying this tactic.

"So can we talk?" Angelica yelled out.

The vamps smiled but said no words yet. Angelica was just about to try again when she saw a vamp behind Zinda, about to attack. She moved quickly to rush him, throwing him on the tracks. Zinda then began shooting, shooting one in the face instantly. Angelica jumped down and smashed the last vamp's head on the tracks. They looked at each other and then around one more time to regroup.

"So how do you think the talk went? Get any useful information?" Zinda blurted out sarcastically.

"Oh, shut up. Well, Ward was right about the small nest here though." Right then, three female vamps emerged from the dark area of the subway. "SHIT!" Angelica yelled out to Zinda.

The middle vamp rushed Angelica slickly across the room like a flash of light, grabbing her neck, and slammed her against the wall, cracking it. The other two replicate the move and slam Zinda to the wall by each of her arms.

Angelica grunted, trying to move. "This is impossible! What the fuck are you?" Slowly emerging from the shadows, a woman walked out from a short distance.

Zinda looked confused at her height. "Damn, she's tall. She's got to be like six feet four," she said, shaking her head.

"Yeah, that is a big bitch," Angelica agreed.

As they stared at her, she used her speed, streaking toward Zinda to slap her face three times. She then wiped blood from Zinda's lips to taste it. She smiled and then headed for Angelica.

"I was dying to meet you," the tall female vamp said to Angelica, staring at her one inch from her face with a seductive hiss.

"What, why?" Angelica asked confusedly but realized she needed more information. "How are you vamps changing so fast?"

"You noticed our power-up?" the tall female vamp replied with pride.

"It's hard not to notice. What changed? What's the endgame for all of this?" Angelica carried on.

"Step one is elimination of the special unit. But don't worry about anything after that because you won't be here to see it," the tall vamp explained, pacing back and forth in slow motion.

"This is stupid. She is not going to tell us anything. I'm done," Zinda replied to them all.

Zinda closed her eyes, reopened them, and her iris started glowing into a purple haze. Purple electricity surged through her arms and into the vamps that are holding her. They screamed as their heads exploded.

There was no time in between when Angelica kicked the tall vamp, pushing her backward. She then ripped off the arm of the other who was holding her down. The vamp screamed, and Angelica punched her through the mouth.

Angelica accelerated with high-speed movement to the tall female vamp who was still on the ground. She jumped on top of her to open her mouth. She stretched it to show her teeth and bit her throat, ripping it out, but ten more vampires came out of the dark to attack.

Zinda took her duster off and gave it to Angelica. "Cover up!"

Angelica covered herself, and Zinda's eyes glowed brighter, making a circle with her hands. It opened a portal above the vamps that flooded the subway with sunlight. The vamps started screaming and burning until smoke was lifting into the portal. They were gone and she closed it. Zinda grabbed her duster and put it back on.

"You could have done that a while back," Angelica said with sarcasm.

"You wanted to talk, remember?" Zinda responded with a nod and smile. Angelica offered a sarcastic smile in return.

"Ward told me to wait until they were all in one spot," Zinda explained further.

"Well, no normals are around, so we're good now. Let's go," Angelica instructed.

"Good, we can do the report in the morning then."

"Sounds good," Angelica said and nodded to agree.

They started to put all of their gear back in place and walked toward their cop vehicles when Zinda realized something. "Wait, why did she want to meet you? Did you know her?"

"No, I didn't know her. She probably always wanted to meet because I used to be a vamp queen. That's why I'm the only Special Unit detective that didn't get announced, and every vamp that sees me, we have to make sure dies."

"Wow, that wasn't in your file," Zinda sighed in disbelief.

"Well, let's go." Angelica nodded and put the car in gear.

Day 3

The clock said 3:00 a.m. as William stared into the night from his office window, on the phone with someone.

"Yes, I know about the vamps' power-up, but it's not a big deal. Goodbye," William said with a stern voice, slamming the phone down. He got up to fix up his suit and grabbed his car keys. The underground parking lot was empty, and the shadows from the dark areas barely gave off any light as he approached his car, but before he got in, four vamps came out from behind him.

"Hello, Mr. Mayor." A hissing vamp started to speak. William turned quickly to look at him. "We wanted you to join us," the vamp continued.

"Really, what does that entail, exactly?" William asked, seeming interested.

"Just a couple of days of discomfort and a small bite," the vamp replied.

"That sounds nice, but I'll pass," William said with no emotion.

"Well, then, I guess we will have to persuade you," the vamp said with another hiss.

"I don't think turning me is worth your life, but let's begin!" William responded, stepping back an inch.

Two vamps head in first to attack. William quickly front kicked one, sending him into a pillar, and caught the other one by the neck. The vamp tried to bite, but he grabbed the vamp's teeth and pulled them out, ripping off the top of his head. The next two jumped in seconds later, kicking him into the hood of a car. One vamp immediately jumped on William, but he caught him and slammed him through the car windshield. He quickly used the broken glass to cut off the head of the vamp he slammed inside.

William jumped off the hood, looking at the last two vamps who regrouped. "Last chance," he said, but they only hissed and stared, waiting.

William rushed and punched one in the side of the face, sending out a shockwave that turned the vamp's head completely around, killing him as he landed back to the ground. He quickly punched the other almost simultaneously, causing another shockwave. He then grabbed the vamp's shirt and picked him up over his head, slamming him over his knee, breaking his back. The vamp screamed as he dropped to the floor, but he didn't die immediately.

"All right, so you are the last one. I only have one question. What the hell is going on with the vamps. Where is this power coming from?" William asked him as he drew in closer.

The vamp tries to talk as he is choking on his own blood. "Philario…Royce…Blood…"

"Okay, now I think I understand." William spoke out loud, but the vamp was gone. He noticed when he looked down and smashed his head in for one last victory hit. After fixing his jacket and tie, he got in his car as if it never happened, but he knew he needed to make a stop.

*****

Philiverse was thumping. Half-naked girls surrounded Tank and the other bouncers, trying to get inside. Every futuristic car was pulling up with extravagant men and women coming out of them. And William pulled up in between them as if they didn't matter.

"Hey, man! What the fuck are you doing?" one man in white suit said in a Spanish accent, but William ignored him and walked up to Tank with a nod.

"Hello, Tank, I need to talk to Philario."

"Hey, Mr. Mayor. Do you have an appointment?" Tank stated with a direct tone.

"No, but you can tell him I'm here now," William suggested.

Tank pushed a button on his radio. "Philario, Mayor is here to see you. He says it's important."

Philario radioed in, "Escort him in."

Tank flagged down the other bouncers to watch the door as he suggested a "come in" with his flexed muscular arm to William, but before this, four armed guards escorted William from behind as he followed Tank.

Once they reached the office, Philario was standing there with his hands in his pockets. "What can I do for you?"

"I won't waste your time. What did you do with the vamps, Philario?" William demanded without sitting or moving.

Philario had a seat and asked William to join, but William declines. "I don't know what you are talking about," Philario said with a sigh.

"Listen, I know you have a small army of your own, but do you really think you can take the NJPD like this?" William asked rhetorically.

"Okay, okay. I was asked by someone to enhance the power of the vamps."

"Why my bloodline?" William asked in a low tone, but angrily.

"Your son was specifically named. In fact, he wanted to only give a small boost, not really overpower them. But as we all know, the vamps can take this power and do what they will, and they chose to get aggressive," Philario explained.

"By who?" William was now more curious than ever.

"I know you're a badass, William. And it's very possible you could whip my ass, but there's no doubt in my mind he could kill me."

"And you expect me to believe that you didn't use some for yourself?" William asked. Philario looked William in the eyes but only smiled.

William sighed, "You know I should kill you now."

Tank picked up his sledgehammer, and the armed guards raised their guns, but Philario raised his hand, and everyone dropped their weapons. He then proceeded to walk around his desk and got into William's face. William had no intention of waiting. He threw a punch, causing a shockwave that knocked pictures off the wall, suddenly cracking windows and chairs in half.

Philario caught his punch and stood there after shape-shifting into William's body. William clinched his eyebrows, shocked.

"Oh yes, I used your blood too." William stepped back.

"What you don't know is that when I shape-shift, I also get the person's ability," Philario explained.

33

William took a deep breath and decided to leave. The guard moved to the side, and even though William didn't look back, he could hear Philario's voice. "If it makes you feel better, there is no more synthesized blood. So the vamps that are left are all that there is." It sounded like an echo, and William made no facial expression to acknowledge it.

Day 4

A press conference was being held outside of city hall and the mayor's office. William is standing in his perfectly pressed suit with a smile over a podium.

"Good morning, good people of New Jericho. All of you might have heard we are having a small vamp problem. So until the NJPD gets it under control, there will be a citywide curfew. Starting today, everyone must be inside by sundown," William stated and nodded his head.

"Do you have any time frame on how long this will be going on?" one Reporter stated, pointing their microphone toward William.

"Unfortunately, no. We just know that the NJPD is doing everything that they can. The special unit is working around the clock."

"Well, no one has heard from your son, Royce, in days. Do you know where he is, and is he okay?" another reporter blurted out.

"To be honest, I unfortunately think that the NJPD special unit was too much for him. In fact, I believe he gave it his best, but he was a little in over his head," William responded.

*****

An old television set was loudly playing the press conference that William was on. Royce was on all fours, sweating and breathing hard with Radd standing over him.

"Did you hear that, boy?" Radd sarcastically antagonized.

Royce pushed himself to stand, determined to look up toward the TV.

34

"Again!" Royce yelled out.

*****

The conference was ending, but William signaled to take one more question.

"The NJPD will be out tracking and killing stray vamps. So anyone that's not a vamp will be risking their life. No more questions." He walked off the platform.

*****

Many homeless people were walking around in a rural area of the city. Some of the lights were out, and the buildings had a ton of graffiti, and trash was just about in every spot. Milo and Buster were patrolling the area for the evening.

"I hate this part of town. Why do you think they always give us this side?" Buster asked Milo.

"Ward said it's this side of town that vamp activity has been happening the most. We need the muscle down here, Buster."

"That's a fucking management answer." Buster rolled his eyes.

"Besides, we need to test the new ammo that Gears and Zinda made," Milo continued as he checked out the window in the darkest areas as they drove slowly through.

A loud scream echoed. Buster pulled over, and they ran around the corner as they saw a vamp attacking a homeless woman. Buster pulled out his gun and aimed.

"Don't you fucking do it," Buster yelled.

"You will kill me no matter what I do!" The vamp held the woman by her neck and proclaimed not to care.

"Yes, you're right," Milo said with sarcasm.

The vampire went in to bite her, and Buster took the shot, hitting the vamp in the head. The vamp started screaming as light came out of his eyes, mouth, and nose, and the woman ran. He dropped to the ground and started burning from inside out of his mouth, fizzling down the rest of his body.

"Holy shit!" Milo yelled, stunned.

"Gears's new bullets charged with a sunlight spell. It is almost like what Zinda can do," Buster said and assumed.

Milo walked back to get on his radio.

"To all members of the NJPD, the ammo is a go!" Milo spoke in the speaker with a smile.

Suddenly, a couple of vampires came out of the shadows and ran away. Milo and Buster tried to shoot them in the back, and when they finally hit, it caused the same effect.

"This is fantastico!" Buster tried to sound excited in Spanish with a little jump in his hip, even though he couldn't speak a word of it.

"Yeah, it's cool, but I like the crushing feeling of their skulls in my hand or under my feet more," Milo sarcastically said as he demonstrated with a smile.

"You read my mind," Buster said as he looked back at Milo.

*****

Ward was sitting at his desk on the phone with all the members of the special unit standing in his office.

"Yes, Mayor, we should be done soon. I'll let you know when you should lift the curfew." Goodbye," Ward said as he shut down the phone.

"How did it go?" Van asked, noticing the conversation was too short.

"We just need to wrap this up as soon as possible. Hey, is your projector working yet?" Ward responded and asked.

"Yeah. It's good."

"Okay, guys, Van takes the lead tonight. This shit needs to end. TONIGHT," Ward demanded.

"I've programmed the satellites to look for vamp DNA," Van informed the group.

"So you can see me now?" Angelica stepped forward.

"Yes, I can see you, but I'm not worried *about you*. It shows one more nest in the warehouse district," Van stated as he activated the holoscreen to show everyone from his arm. Angelica looked up and then again to the floor. Ward noticed.

"All right, load up. We leave in ten," Van ordered. Everyone grabbed their gear and headed out.

"Hold on, Van," Ward said as he was the last one out. "Be careful. I'm reading fear from Angelica. And you know what that means."

"I'll keep an eye on her," Van promised.

"If you think she might flip on you, I give you the go-ahead to kill her."

"Yes, sir," Van said without emotion.

CHAPTER 5

The Flying Vamp

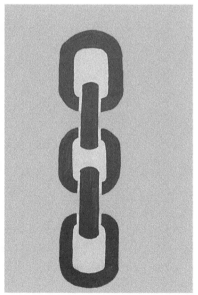

Over twelve cop cars pulled up to an abandoned warehouse. As everybody exited the vehicles, they heard screeching from the vamps coming from the inside.

Van signaled to gather and listen.

"All normals surround the building, and shoot anything that moves. Special unit, pick a building or rooftop and keep watch," Van ordered as he pointed in different directions.

"What the hell are you about to do, Van?" Milo asked. Van looked at Milo and gestured to move out.

"Let me help with that. Just tell me what the plan is," Zinda butted in before Milo walked off.

"Please, just do what I ask." Van didn't have time to explain.

Van already knew that they were going to encounter a battle with twenty vamps. He had detected it earlier, but he didn't want to frighten anyone.

They all went to take their positions. When Angelica got to her side of the building, she saw a dark figure standing on the edge, watching everything. He was wearing black combat boots, a black hoodie, and a black bandanna over his face.

"You shouldn't be here!" Angelica yelled out to him. But the man stayed silent. "Who are you?" Angelica sensed uneasiness. She then saw three dead vamps lying on the floor behind him. She decided to pull her gun and point.

"Last chance to answer. Who the hell are you?"

*****

Van was pushing the buttons on his holoscreen and took cover behind a car. A huge red glowing beam rained down, engulfing the building as everyone covered their eyes from the light, which now also took over the night sky, accumulating sounds of thunder.

*****

Angelica thought she was alone when she saw the figure. The light made her cover her eyes. She tried hard to squint to focus on the figure, but he was gone.

*****

Van looked again at the holoscreen. All twenty vamps that were originally in the building had disappeared. *Wait...that's impossible,* Van thought.

"There still has to be one more!" Van yelled out to his crew. "WAIT!"

Everyone stayed silent, waiting.

Behind the ruins, a ten-foot vamp with wings burst out, sending debris in all directions. His wings struck some of the NJPD normals, knocking them down and cutting some normals instantly in half.

"Holy shit! Normals, evacuate! Evacuate!" Van yelled, screaming over and over to whoever was left.

Buster and Milo immediately transformed. They waited for the vamp to fly closer. They tackled him down to the ground before he cut another normal in half. They clawed at him, but they barely left any marks. The vamp grabbed both of them by the neck as his wings engulfed them, slamming them against each other, then tossing them aside.

Van could see from a distance. He immediately turned his holoscreen on but then realized that it needed to recharge.

Zinda's heartbeat started to race, trying to concentrate so she could help. Her eyes started to glow, and she opened up a portal. She flooded the area with sunlight. The beams hit the vampire, causing it to scream and fall to his knees. She was holding it to wait for his image to completely burn. She closed the portal as he became motionless, but his wings started to flap.

"Dad! No!" Angelica yelled out from behind when he flew out toward Zinda. Angelica tried to block him, but it knocked her into Zinda instead. It threw Zinda into the window of the next building. The same power also pushed Angelica through a door that was behind her. Vans looked up and quickly reacted, running over to Angelica.

"Are you okay?" Van asked.

"Yes, but my arm is broken," Angelica answered.

"Did you say 'dad'?" Van asked.

"Yes, he is my father. His name is Fane," Angelica stated but looked away when she answered.

"We have to take him down. Is this going to be a problem, Angelica?"

"No," Angelica stated with a ripple in her voice, looking Van in the eyes to assure him.

"Good. You're the only one fast enough to follow him. When he stops, you have to give us the location," Van ordered.

Angelica got up, pushed her arm back into place, and streaked. Fane is flying with the dark figure on the rooftop, chasing him. The figure caught up and leaped onto his back. Fane started flying in circles, trying to roll him off. He then flew backwards into a billboard. The mysterious man fell but hung on to his wing, using his strength to pull himself back up and started to tear his wing.

Fane screamed in pain as it started detaching, being torn off completely. After that, he threw the wing to the ground, and it stuck in the ground like a sword, just missing Angelica as she started to catch up.

Fane started to fall and crashed with the mystery man into a parking lot, destroying most of the cars. They slowly got up.

"How dare you do this to me! I have lived through three resets. You can't do this!" Fane yelled out when he suddenly flung toward the mystery man who dodges yet still endures a cut on his chest which angers him. He runs at Fane, jumping and kicking him over a car and into another one. Then he kicked a car, and it slid into Fane, trapping him. The man stood there watching as Fane struggled to move the car and stood up but fell to the ground. The man walked over, grabbed his wing, and put his foot on his back, then ripped off his other wing. Fane screamed and tried to crawl away.

The man walked over with his severed wing and, without a word, chopped off his head.

Angelica stood there watching from a short distance and stopped running to take in her father's death. "Goodbye, Father." She then grabbed her mic on her gear to report with a tear.

"Van, it's done. I'm sending you my location. And there is someone helping, someone strong, and I don't know who or what he is."

Angelica turned back around again, and the man was gone. Her eyes then focused on her father's dead body. She sighed with a tear but then noticed a strange smell in the air.

*****

The next morning, outside the mayor's office, the NJPD was being honored by the mayor. A large crowd had gathered to hear his speech.

"I'm glad to inform you that the vamp problem is over. Thanks to the NJPD, I am going to lift the curfew. We can finally get back to normal," William said as he gripped his suit to adjust it, waving and nodding at the crowd.

*****

Royce drove up to Radd's shop and waltzed in. He was sitting down, patiently waiting for him. "Well, well, your body seemed to accept the chain durability tattoo. You didn't have to try so hard to test it," Radd said.

"There was no other way," Royce said with a sigh. "Getting my ass kicked was the only way?"

Radd ignored the comment.

"And the running man tat for agility is amazing too!" Royce boasted.

"You made a good choice on these guns and their names," Radd suggested.

"Reign. Yeah, I like it. Snow is the other," Royce responded, still looking down at the two guns he selected.

Royce planted the guns inside his shoulder holsters under his coat. Deep down he wanted to thank Radd but instead looked around as if he had nothing left to say.

"Well, that will be all," Radd said, instructing Royce to walk out to his vehicle.

When Royce's eyes pierced down the street, he saw the same figure standing on a building not too far away. It was the same figure during the announcement of his position with the NJPD.

"Hey, see that guy standing there?" Royce pointed for Radd to notice.

Radd turned to look around but didn't see anything. He looked back at Royce, confused. "No. You okay? You seeing things now?"

"Nah, never mind."

"So what is happening first? You going to check in with the NJPD now?" Radd asked.

"No, I gotta make a pit stop first," Royce explained.

*****

Royce walked into the atrium at city hall. He looked around through a crowd of people when he finally saw William at the top of the steps. He was talking to other members of the board.

"William, we need to talk!" Royce yelled out.

"Everyone please welcome my son. Looks like he's all healed up and ready to work again," William said with a fake smile. Everyone in the atrium started clapping and facing his direction.

"EVERYONE SHUT THE FUCK UP AND GET OUT!" Royce unexpectedly yelled toward the crowd. But nobody moved because they went frozen, not expecting that.

William immediately took the floor again.

"Everyone please take the rest of the day off. We need a father-and-son talk," William said and then turned to Royce with a stone-cold face. The people scattered to the exit, and William gestured to Royce to follow him to his office.

"Get down here, William. I'm going to show you why this will be the last time you're going to underestimate me," Royce demanded, facing him.

William walked slowly down the stairs, removing his suit jacket.

"I know we don't have a strong relationship, and I know a lot of it is my fault. But I am still your father, and you will respect me," William demanded.

"We will see," Royce stated as they did not take their eyes off each other.

"Just remember, kid, you left the family. We didn't kick you out," William reminded.

They finally met face-to-face, and the stares became more intense.

William decided to throw an unexpected punch. Royce caught his fist, sending a shock wave through the hall, allowing him to kick William's feet from underneath him, causing him to fall. Royce proceeded to again kick him in the chest, sliding him across the room. As William's back hit the wall, he stood back up but was holding on to his side.

"I see you've gotten stronger," William said with sarcasm.

But without a second thought, William rushed Royce, throwing punches. They were all blocked except the last punch to the stomach. The shock waves knocked all the pictures off the wall.

William tried to pull back, but Royce was holding on to his arm. Royce hit William with four straight right hands to the face, again sending shock waves, moving benches and chairs abruptly across the room. He then gave a front kick to William, making him yell in yearning pain, causing his back to hit the stairs. He slowly got up, and Royce was standing over him to punch him. But William grabbed Royce by the neck and picked him up to slam into the ground, cracking the floor. William stomped on Royce's chest, sending shock waves, adding cracks to the floor. This gave him the advantage to pick Royce up to smash him through the pillars. The concrete fell on his head and back, also sending William backward, causing Royce, with tremendous force, to slide backward.

"What the fuck is your problem, Royce?" William asked as they could not stand or move after the impact.

"Do you think I'm ever gonna forgive how you treated Mom and me? The cheating, the absence, the neglect. Then caring for other kids, as if I never existed," Royce clarified.

"Royce, you're still a child. You don't understand. And you're too soft. You're not strong enough to walk the path I wanted you to. I had to invest in others," William said as he slowly stood up and walked over, limping.

"I'm sorry I hurt you, kid, but you had it coming. If it helps, you fucked up my back, and I'm pretty sure you broke some ribs," William admitted.

Royce started to heal as he stood there breathing, starting to stretch. "What the fuck? How can you even move?" William was astounded.

Royce grabbed William and kneed him in the stomach. Twice. Then uppercut him, causing a shock wave that blew through the windows, lifting him six feet off the ground and then causing him to fall hard to the ground.

Royce reached toward him, but William was frozen on the ground.

"If you can't defend yourself anymore, then let me help you," Royce finally said.

Royce bent down and fixed William's tie. "There you go."

Some city hall workers were watching as the entire thing went down. Royce turned around and walked out right past them. They were frozen and didn't dare move as he went by.

"Give your mayor some help," Royce instructed the workers as he walked out.

Later that day, Royce arrived at the NJPD.

"Welcome back, Royce," Van greeted him at the door, tipping his head as if he had a hat on. "Thanks, it's good to be back. Did I miss anything?"

Before Van could answer, Ward was yelling from the back of the building in his office, "Everyone in my office now!"

Everyone froze and turned around to slowly walk in that direction.

"Good job on the vamp issue, everyone. Sorry you missed it, Royce. It would have been good training for you."

"Sorry I missed it too," Royce replied from the center of the crowd.

"I know it's late, but this is our team. You know Van, this is Milo, Buster, Zinda, and Angelica. This is your team." They all nodded when Buster walked up to Royce to size him up. "The rest of the crew is just normal and helps in the other departments."

"Just to let you know, no one cares that you killed a vamp barehanded. We all do that all the time." Buster had to say something sarcastic.

Milo decided to join in, "Yeah, and where were you when we just killed a couple of hundred within the last five days?"

"Hey, fluffy snowball, what the fuck is your problem? Royce nodded to each as he asked with no fear.

"How dare you bring our mothers into this!" Buster yelled. Ward walked closer toward them to cool it down.

"Hey, guys, chill, there's no way that he could have known that was your mother's names," Ward said, coming in between them to hand out some files that were on his desk.

"Milo, Buster, there have been a few kidnappings lately. I need you to look into that," Ward instructed.

"Wait, wouldn't that be for the normals?" Milo asked.

"Yes, normally, but they are disappearing without a trace, so the case hit my desk. That means it's you guys now. Angelica, Zinda, I need you to patrol for the next week. See if you can find any stray vamps and take care of them. Lastly, Royce, Van, we have an arsonist running around our city, and we need to find him as soon as possible."

Ward dismissed everybody as they were gathering in the lobby to watch the TV. The breaking news came on. William was on TV with his face swollen, in crutches, with his arm in a sling.

"I don't want anybody to worry, I'm okay. Business should go on as usual," William announced over the PA system.

"City hall workers are saying it was your son Royce that did this to you. Is there any truth to that? a reporter asked.

"What happened is a family matter, not a mayor or city matter. My son and I will work this out privately, and I'm not going to be taking any more questions on personal matters."

Everyone turned to look at Royce with strange stares. "What?" Royce asked with annoyance.

"Who does their dad like that?" Zinda asked with a smirk.

"We're just lucky he's not making the NJPD pay for the damage to the city hall," Ward put in his two cents from the back of the crowd.

"Let's go, Van, we got an arsonist to catch," Royce said, looking at Van, trying to leave as quickly as possible.

Royce and Van started to walk out and Angelica watched them, staring.

Van instructed Royce to drive.

"How the hell are we going to find an arsonist?" Royce opened the door, waiting for Van to answer.

"We can examine the fires, look for some patterns. We may get some clues."

The driving seemed endless when Royce spotted a figure on the roof of a building to the left of him. As he clenched his eyes together to take a better look, he blinked. But the figure was then gone.

"I think I'm seeing things."

"What? Why do you say that?" Van asked.

"Because I keep—"

"Wait," Van sternly interrupted. "It's going to have to wait. Look ahead, that building is on fire."

"Well, that's convenient," Royce responded as he stepped on the gas.

"Yes, it is, but let's be careful," Van instructed.

They pulled over as they reached the building. They got out slowly to look around first when a woman suddenly ran up to them.

"I think there are kids in there!" She slightly raised her voice out of panic.

"Okay, get back to a safe distance," Van instructed. She stayed behind not too far back, watching for a minute.

They got ready to pull their guns out, moving forward, keeping their eyes focused on the building. As they pressed on, the woman ran to turn the corner behind another building, suddenly shape-shifting back into Philario.

"I'll go in. I can take the heat better than you can," Royce suggested to Van.

"Okay, just be careful."

"Aww, you're so sweet, you know that?" Royce wanted to give Van a taste of his own sarcasm.

"Just go!" Van smirked.

Royce ran in the burning building, ran up the stairs when he heard screams. He got to the fifth floor, and the hallway walls were on fire. Royce ran down the hall into an open room. He saw walls on fire and two girls sitting in a chair, tied up. A young kid stood between them with shoulder-length dreads, untucked red button shirt, black pants, and red sneakers, with his hands in his pocket.

"Hello, big brother, I think it's time we've talked."

CHAPTER 6

The Brother

H e looked at Royce straight in the eyes, expecting his shock.

"Hello, Cincere, I was wondering when you would pop up," Royce proclaimed.

"It's just Cin now."

"Well, you've gotten big," Royce said as if he was talking to his younger brother with pride.

"Well, that's what eight years will do to you. You would have seen it if you weren't a bitch and left your little brother behind."

"Oh, poor prodigy. You were fine with William all alone. I knew he would die before he let anything happen to his prodigy."

"I didn't care about that. I just wanted my big brother, but you left," Cin recanted.

"You were too young to understand anything," Royce tried to explain while holding his gun steady in Cin's direction.

"I've been watching you for a while, Royce, and I'm over it. You are strong enough to join us now."

Royce noticed the fire getting worse. And the girls were frozen, scared. "What? Join this evil?" Royce asked.

Cin looked around and laughed.

"Evil? What evil are you talking about?"

"The fire and the girls that are tied up next to you, is this the way you do things?" Royce stopped for a second, realizing something. "Wait, you started all these fires, Cin? The kidnappings, the arsonists, and I suppose these are your abilities?" Royce asked again.

"Yes, but all the people I have kidnapped are safe. I just wanted to talk, and I will return all of them. It's not my fault the NJPD took so long to start looking into it."

"Was that you on all the buildings I've been seeing? Disappearing in front of my eyes? I thought I was going fucking crazy," Royce admitted.

"It's not my fault you forgot about my ability. I'll make sure you won't forget again," Cin recanted.

Cin disappeared, and then reappeared in front of Royce. Punched him in the face before he could react. He continued to teleport, hitting him each time. The last punch put Royce in a daze that he could barely hold on his gun.

"Wow, you've gotten fast, but you lack power," Royce said, getting his stamina back.

"Lack power?" Cin repeated with anger.

He ran at Royce, teleporting to kick him in the face, sending Royce sliding back against the floor, but Royce immediately stood back up.

"Like I said, evil," Royce recanted.

"I've come to terms with my demons but I guess not my evil." Cin's body started to smoke as he raised his hands and snapped his fingers.

Royce looked confused. "What the fuck?" He was suddenly engulfed by flames. "No!" he screamed. But Royce wasn't burning. Cin stared trying to burn him more, but nothing. Cin looked confused.

"What the hell? How are you doing that?" Cin asked.

Royce realized he felt nothing and stopped yelling.

Cin teleported behind Royce and kicked him in the back. Royce immediately turned to kick back, hitting Cin in the stomach, sending him out a window. As he was flying outward, he teleported to save himself and sucked all the fire into the teleportation with him.

Royce walked over to the girls as the fire department pulled up. You could hear the noises and the relief from the girls' voices. He escorted them out where he saw Van coming to the door.

They put the girls in the truck when Royce looked up to see Cin on the building across the street. When he blinked, he was gone.

"So are you going to tell me what happened in there? How did you put the fire out so quickly? I couldn't get past the doors," Van asked.

"I had a quick family reunion, but I didn't put it out," Royce answered, still looking around for Cin.

"Well, it looks like you tried," Van said, pointing to Royce's clothes.

Royce took a look at his clothes, realizing he had a lot of damage from the fire on him. "Damn!" Royce grunted.

"We need to get back to the office," Van instructed.

"What the hell happened to you?" Ward blurted out with a confused look on his face since Royce didn't look in the best condition.

Royce shook his head. "Nothing. The arsonist is done, and the kidnapping is done too. The victims should be home shortly."

"All right, but I need your report by tomorrow," Ward sternly said without emotion.

Royce looked back at Ward directly in the eyes. "Sorry, Ward, not this time," he said as he walked out.

*****

Inside William's office, he was sitting at his desk fiddling with a gadget on his desk, contemplating, when Cin teleported in. He immediately threw up into the trash can close by.

"Whatever happened to you?" William asked, ignoring the throwing up.

Cin lifted up his head to look directly at his father when he noticed his crutch and arm sling. "What happened to me? What happened to you?" Cin recanted.

"What, you don't catch the news?" William said sarcastically.

"I'm thirteen years old. I don't care about the news."

"I'll just say your brother is stronger than I thought," William sighed while trying to get up from his chair.

"Royce did that to you?"

"Yes, and you?" William asked, already knowing the answer.

"Yes, him too, but he just got lucky. He's nothing. I'm a prodigy," Cin spoke with confidence after the smell of vomit in his mouth was gone.

"Yes, your power is amazing, but you're a marshmallow. You can't take a hit, son. And all power in the world means nothing if you get hit once and it's over," William tried to explain in a fatherly tone.

"I said he was lucky," Cin argued.

"If you say so," William responded sarcastically

"I have a question. I set him on fire, but he didn't burn. Why?" Cin asked but was surprised at William's response.

"Are you fucking serious? You set your brother on fire?" William was more shocked that he did it.

"Yes, but like I said, he didn't burn."

"Yazmin," William rhetorically stated.

"What about Mom?"

"She must have done it." Cin just stared, confused at his response.

"I guess you should know. She is the reason you're so different. She was a powerful witch. And even though Royce was born normal for a supernatural, like me, I knew he wouldn't be enough," William tried to explain.

"And me?" Cin pleaded.

"Your mom knew what I was trying to do, so she endowed you with the abilities that you have. But I didn't know she gave it to Royce too. She would have not known what would come to the surface. She did it mostly to protect you both, I'm sure."

"So what was I, an experiment?" Cin asked.

"Yazmin must have put a protection spell on Royce. When your fire ability surfaced. So I guess your fire won't affect him after all," William said with his eyes phasing in a daze.

"Dad!" Cin blurted out intensely, looking upset.

William looked back at Cin. "Heal slow," he said as he teleported away.

*****

Van and Royce again were patrolling the city. Royce was exhausted but held out on saying anything until…

"Can you take me home?"

Van turned to answer, but then a dispatch came over the radio, "Van, we got a DV issue. I sent it to your GPS."

A stroke of adrenaline went through both of them. "Let's hit it!" Van yelled out.

"Man, I'm tired. Our shift is over," Royce recanted.

"We can go home if you tell me what happened in the building," Van bribed him.

Royce took a deep breath and loaded the GPS instead. They pulled up to an apartment building with a man standing in front of the entrance as they walked up.

"Excuse me, but we need you to move," Van instructed the man.

"Why don't you get out of here? My friend isn't doing anything," the man answered with anger.

"We got a domestic violence call. We need to talk to your friend."

"Mind your fucking business, cops!" the man said, getting in Van's face, putting a finger onto Van's forehead, but Van grabbed his hand and bent it backward.

"You got this?" Royce asked from a distance without interfering.

"Yeah, go ahead," Royce instructed to walk through.

Royce walked past both of them and went into the building. The man yelled as Van practically broke his arm, putting it behind his back.

The yelling turned into a yelp and then a sudden horrific growl. The man suddenly turned into a werewolf.

Van let go and jumped back. "HOLY SHIT!"

The werewolf tore off a piece of Van's coat, then lunged at Van for a second time, but Van ducked, and the claws ripped into Royce's truck.

"Fuck!" Van yelled out and pressed his vest for backup.

Van pulled two darts from his back belt and threw one, hitting the werewolf in the chest. The werewolf howled to yank the darts out of his chest with all his strength and then charged Van. But he stumbled, and Van saw his opportunity to rush in. He then kicked him in the knee, which broke the werewolf's left side, making him growl in pain. Van grabbed the dart off the floor and quickly stabbed him in the neck. The werewolf dropped to the ground when Milo and Buster finally pulled up and transformed.

Howling and glass breaking was coming from the distance. "Oh, shit! Royce!" Van yelled out.

Royce landed on the roof of his truck, smashing it on his back. Milo and Buster looked at each other and let out a laugh.

"Damn, Van, you could have told me they're werewolves," Royce directed to Van out of breath. "And what the fuck are you guys laughing at?" he said as he was moving left to right, trying to get backup.

"No! My baby!" Royce realized he landed on his truck. He cuddled his face in agony.

Royce jumped up and ran around his truck, then into the building while Milo and Buster were laughing in their wolf growls, and Van was trying not to laugh. Then Royce ran back into the building, and they heard the sounds of a dog crying. A werewolf fell out the window and hit the ground with a broken leg, arm, and his bottom jaw broken and hanging. Van took a dart and stabbed him in the back. He turned back and fainted. Royce jumped out the window, sat on the curb next to his smashed truck. Milo and Buster were still laughing.

"Can you believe he is crying?" Milo hit Buster on his chest to agree.

"His baby…his baby," Buster mocked.

"Royce, I'll call gears for you," Van put his arm around his shoulders.

"Fuck this shit!" Royce yelled out. "Wait, Gears? Oh, all right," Royce said, calming down but shaking his head.

*****

The next morning, Royce walked into the precinct, thinking about his baby. He looked at no one, determined to get to the auto department. His truck was there but still smashed. Royce produced a disappointed smirk on his face when he heard a TV playing cartoons and someone laughing.

"Gears!" Royce called out.

The chair looked empty, but it turned around, and there was a blond-haired skinny young kid in it. He had huge glasses that made his eyes look big with a wifebeater muscle shirt on with black jeans and black boots.

"Hey, kid, your dad here?" Royce asked.

"Why would my dad be here? I'm Gears."

"What? You're like eight!"

"I'm twelve, jerk."

"Are you serious?" Royce thought for a moment. "Well, look, kid, just tell me how long it will be."

"Well, there's a cartoon marathon on, so maybe I'll get it done in two days," Gears replied with sarcasm. Gears grabbed a bowl of cereal and turned back around to watch the cartoons. Royce shook his head and decided to go check in with the rest of the precinct.

Angelica walked in from the basement stairs as he was exiting the body shop.

"Hello, Gears," Angelica called out.

"Hey, Angelica!" Gears seemed excited to see her when he jumped out of his chair. "What can I do for you?" He looked desperate to help.

"I need to look at Royce's truck, okay?"

"Why?" Gears questioned with no expression.

"Why is that important?"

Gears stared for a minute. "Well, I'll do anything if you let me." He then put his hand out to try to touch the side of her hip.

"If you touch me again, I'll slap you through this wall."

"Man! Why do you have to always ruin my day?" Gears grunted like a child. Gears started to watch TV again.

She stared at Gears for a second, then walked over to the truck and shook her head at the severe damage on the truck. She saw a drop of blood, smelled it, and seemed shocked at the taste of it. She looked to see if Gears saw her, then decided to walk out.

As she was passing Ward's office, he started to yell, "Everyone in here, now." All members walked in, and he turned up the TV near his entrance. William was talking to a reporter.

"So, Mr. Mayor, it's that time of the year again, and the city wants to know what you were going to do about it?"

"I'm aware of the time of the year," William answered sarcastically.

The reporter decided to immediately try another approach. "Yes, but the blood moon is in two days. What is the plan?"

"I'm in cahoots with Ward at the head of NJPD. We are all about putting this to an end. Not to worry."

"Can we ask what plans you two are discussing?" the reporter probed.

"Well, if you must know, I'm thinking of a kill order. But I will give you a definite answer before the blood moon rises though." William nodded his head when Ward turned the TV off.

"I need to go before the sun comes up," Angelica directed in general toward the room.

Ward waved her off without looking at her to direct the conversation to the rest. She nodded but didn't leave before staring at Royce up and down. Zinda took notice but went back to paying attention to Ward.

"I've seen blood moons before, and there are a lot of werewolves out. But what's the real problem?" Royce asked as they started to discuss.

"This guy." Milo pointed his thumb to Royce.

"What was that?" Royce retaliated.

"Enough! You guys act like a bunch of kids," Ward interfered.

"There are werewolves that can change at will like us," Buster answered.

"And they can change only at night, or at the full moon," Milo continued with sarcasm in Royce's direction.

"Then some can only change on a blood moon," Buster finished the explanation.

"So they are stronger than any other werewolves?" Royce probed more with eyebrows drawn and nodded to be sarcastic.

Van nodded at Royce as he walked out. When Royce reached the hallway alone, Zinda had followed him from behind. She grabbed his arm. "Hey, I don't know what you did to Angelica, but she has a problem."

"I kind of figured that, but like you said, that's her problem." Royce pulled his arm back.

"Okay, don't say I didn't warn you," Zinda said before walking off.

Van finally caught up noticing the encounter. "Let's go," he instructed Royce as he walked past him.

"Are we heading to Philiverse?" Royce asked, following. Van nodded yes.

CHAPTER 7

The Other Weres in Town

Milo and Buster were driving when a dispatch called in directly to them.

"There is a disturbance at the Jericho Cuisine. Check it out," the sexy voice relayed over.

Milo's eyebrows went up twice since he had a crush on the hot dispatch chick. Buster smiled and shook his head no.

"We are on our way," Milo responded, sounding nonchalant.

To the right where they parked were two shiny black motorcycles that Milo noticed right away. The Jericho Cuisine was a fancy place, and motorcycles were not usually parked in valet, but then a huge distraction grabbed his attention. Two men were suddenly thrown out of a window, crashing glass everywhere.

"Oh, shit, Grimfurs are back!" Milo turned while letting out a grunt to Buster as if he wasn't surprised.

"Just like clockwork for the blood moon," Buster agreed.

Two men stepped out of the window onto the broken glass, laughing at the men on the ground. The men on the ground were completely annihilated and couldn't pick up their heads to look up.

The first man smirked when he finally turned to see Milo and Buster standing there. "Oh, look, NJPD's werewolves."

They cleaned up their attire and decided to walk over to them. "What can we do for you, Officers?" one spoke first.

But before Milo and Buster could answer, one immediately partially shifted into a werefox and sneered with his teeth showing. The other into a weredog, resembling a very large rottweiler. They jumped toward Buster and Milo, snarling and snapping at them. The weredog grabbed Milo by the neck, picking him up and slamming him against the wall when the werefox bit Buster on the shoulder. Buster transformed but still couldn't push the werewolf off before Milo was able to, but when he finally did, he was able to reach an angle to kick the weredog into werefox. They both go backward, heading into the wall, smashing some of the concrete. Buster got up and picked up one of the motorcycles to slam it down on them. Milo caught his move quickly and repeated it, slamming them again with the other one.

Milo yelled out to buster, "DISPATCH! Reach out to Van."

Buster stayed to watch them on the ground from attacking back, but they were badly hurt and could barely move, quickly yelping in pain.

"Send in a wagon that can hold wereanimals," Milo spoke into dispatch after transforming back.

Dispatch confirmed when Van also chimed in.

"Van, the Grimfurs are riding around. They can only partially turn because the moon isn't here yet, but they are pretty strong. Be on the lookout."

"Got it, Milo, thanks," Van answered right away.

*****

Van and Royce arrived at Philiverse. The place looked dead. Van looked around, suspicious considering what time it was, but Royce was just disappointed that there were no girls to look at on the way in.

"Where is everyone?" Royce asked with a sad tone as entering the place was a shock.

"Why is everything all fucked up?" Van stated with a confused look, ignoring Royce. Footsteps emerged when Philario and Tank came down from the upper floor.

"Can I help you?" Philario asked with sarcasm.

"What happened here?" Van asked with a little concern even though he wasn't.

"Grimfurs came through, scared my customers off. Killed my gunman. Everyone but Tank," Philario said, pointing to Tank's hammer. "But Tank got most of them."

"Tank *I understand, but you,* don't think so." Royce looked at Tank to antagonize him.

Philario got agitated and shapeshifted into Tank. Royce and Van's eyes lit up with surprise, and Royce took two steps back. "Okay, okay, I will cool it. No need to show off," Royce voiced with a stern tone while clearing his throat.

"Again, what do you want?" Philario said, shifting back into himself.

"Tank," Royce responded.

Van looked over. "What?"

"I think we could use Tank against the Grimfurs," Royce answered.

"I don't think so." Philario immediately rejected the idea.

Van stayed quiet for a minute while leaning against the destroyed bar. "I'm sure there is something you need or want, Philario. Help a guy out," Van tried to negotiate with some childlike play in his voice.

"Wait, why can't Tank answer?" Royce sarcastically asked as if Tank was his buddy.

Tank blew his bad breath that emerged like green smoke in Royce's face. Royce quickly backed away, clearing the air, but almost choked.

"Because I speak for him, but I've been working for Cin, you get me out of that, and I'll let you use Tank." Philario realized this might work.

"Wait, Cin has been the problem the whole time?" Royce asked with anticipation.

"Yes," Philario confirmed.

"Cin? Okay, what the hell is that?" Van asked, not realizing what or who Cin is or was.

"I'll take care of it. See you soon, Tank." Royce ignored Van and started walking out.

"We'll see," Tank responded by waving his hand off with no care.

Van followed him out, but they saw two motorcycles around their vehicle. One man was sitting on the hood, and the other one was leaning on the side.

"What can we do for you, gentlemen?" Van asked as he came closer.

"We've been waiting for the NJPD to show up," the one leaning remarked with soft aggression. Van stared with a blank look on his face.

The second got up and glanced at Royce and Van to finish his sentence. "We've been told to thin out the special unit," he said, threatening.

Van immediately stepped back to draw his gun and, without warning, shot the man in the head. The other man became angry and turned into a werewolf, lunging at Royce, but he dodged. Van jumped on his back with his gun, ready to fire, shooting him in the neck, almost clearing off half his head.

Dammit, Van!" Royce yelled in frustration but was glad he saved him.

"Well, it's just two less that we're going to have to deal with later," Van tried to explain while he clipped the roof of his gun, putting the smoke out.

"This shit never ends." Royce slammed the car door to get in.

*****

Royce and Van arrived at the precinct. The sky looked blue and more orange than normal. Royce started to realize he desperately needed some sleep when he was looking up, but he sighed without complaint and headed in behind Van.

The precinct was loud and busy as usual. Buster was in the corner, getting stitched up. "Hey, what happened to you?" Van asked, walking up, looking concerned.

"We told you, those fuckers are super strong," Buster replied, not looking up, very annoyed.

"Everyone in the office!" Ward yelled out as usual from his doorway, standing with William next to him.

Royce rolled his eyes. "Shit," he said under his breath. Everyone headed over.

"With the members we caught and killed, their leader, Mane, wants to talk," William informed the crew.

"And after William approved the kill order, we have finally killed a few of them," Ward offered more information.

"We saw more that Tank and Philario killed at Philiverse," Van jumped in.

"And don't forget the two outside," Royce added.

"With kill squads on the edge of the city, they're going to know it's over," William suggested.

"You shouldn't go there, Mr. Mayor. They will kill you," Milo sternly said, looking at Ward for support.

"I will be fine. I plan on giving them a pass. Just, let's get them out of the city," William argued.

"Dismissed." Ward ended the conversation.

"Hold on, Royce," Ward stopped him as everyone was leaving.

"William is worried. I think he feels he's going to die tonight. I would feel better if you backed him up," Ward suggested, staring at Royce in the eyes.

"Only if that's an order, Captain," Royce said with distress.

"No, but you are his son." Ward leaned back to sit and started looking at documents on his desk. Royce walked out of his office and didn't look back.

*****

Later that night, William pulled up in a black SUV near an abandoned warehouse. He was met by two men on a motorcycle in all-black suits with helmets that had GRIM on top in orange. One signaled William to follow. They led him to a parking lot between two buildings. William got out to see a huge man sitting on a chopper with four more men half his size on motorcycles. There was one on each side of him. The huge man got off and walked toward William. As William walked forward, the gang behind them stayed frozen.

"So let's get right to it. You guys want safe passage out of the city. I'm willing to give it to you if you make it fast and you make it now," William instructed.

The main guy stared in silence while walking in closer to him until they were five inches apart.

William took a hard look up and down at the six-foot-eight Caucasian male who had a fierce jaw and long hair and thick beard. He was wearing full leather biker gear and had a lean massive physique, but William didn't flinch.

"I'm surprised you showed up," he finally spoke.

"Mane, you said you wanted to talk about you leaving. Are we still on for that?"

"You made that up. All I said was let's talk."

"Okay, let's talk." William threw his hands out slightly to indicate the time was now but slightly stepped back.

"This is our city too. We want the rights that we should have to live here just like anyone else."

"And that would be a great argument if you and your crew didn't destroy everything. This is all because the blood moon is here. And I can't let you do that anymore." William stayed stern in his voice.

"So you think killing my squad is your way of handling the situation?" Mane recanted in a professional tone.

"Look, Mane, I'm just following orders. The truth is he doesn't like your little gang fucking up his city. And he told me to put a stop to it. It's causing more trouble than it's worth, and you know this," William continued to explain.

"Ward," Mane laughs. "Well, maybe we should use you as a message to him," Mane threatened.

Without warning, Mane tightened his fist to jab William on his left cheek, but he caught his arm and flipped Mane over, slamming his shoulder into the ground. Mane stood back up to rush William, gripping him around the waist. William elbowed him in the back, sending a shock wave crushing him to his knees, which also scatters all of the men surrounding them in a backward motion.

"Mane, you can't defeat me," William said in a condescending tone.

"Good, I thought this was going to be boring," Mane said with a smile.

Mane lifted his eyes to William's to begin a sinister laugh as he started to form into a seven-foot tall lion with a roar that seemed to send a vibrating wind through the air.

"Holy shit? A werelion? Oh I get it, Mane. That's good!" William yelled out over the roar.

Mane raised his fists and brought it down on William's shoulder, stomping him into the ground. He then picked him up by the neck, punching him in the stomach twice, slamming him down again.

William coughed up blood.

"Damn! I see why you are the leader," William said sarcastically, acting as if he was not hurt. Mane's claws came out to show his anger.

Right then, a cop car pulled up and Royce emerged as quickly as he could, shocked to see a lion in full form. Two of the men who were able to get back up tried to rush Royce with weapons, but Royce's speed defeated the act quickly by two bullets from one of his Rhinos.

"So I guess talking didn't work?" Royce yelled out to William while still holding his gun up to protect himself.

"Guns! I knew you and your dad were bitches!" Mane insulted.

"Bitches! Well, maybe him, I'm just the backup!" Royce answered sarcastically.

"Both of you together can't beat me!" Mane yelled.

Royce smiled at his pathetic gesture and placed his guns and jacket on the hood of the car. All of the men surrounding looked at Mane to attack Royce. As they come closer to Royce, he punched them both in the face like ragdolls, sliding them across the concrete. The punches were stern enough to cause a shock wave as his eyes pierced on Mane.

"STOP!" Mane yelled out while stepping back to size up Royce. Royce took the opportunity to help William up.

"I knew you would come." William thanked him. Royce took a deep breath and rolled his eyes over.

"Just know he doesn't fight like a were. He fights like a man." William winked to offer Royce some encouragement.

William fixed his gear, pressing it against his body and arms to make sure he was ready. They didn't have much time before he attacked.

The fight began.

William, without another word, turned to Mane's direction and rushed his leg, sweeping him down to the ground. Royce then jumped up and punched him, making him slam his head against concrete. William leaped over in slow motion to lunge onto his back, but he rolled out of the way, moving forward, and he kicked William's back. Royce tried to protect William by grabbing Mane to pick him up, but he dodged and turned to claw and pick up Royce by his neck. Royce got slammed down, landing him near William. William quickly grabbed Royce's leg and pulled him out of the way as Mane tried to stomp on him, allowing him room to kick Mane in the face. Mane stumbled backward but still was able to backhand William, sliding him across the floor. Royce jabbed Mane in the side three times, causing shock waves over and over again within the field. The scene took on a slow motion of pain in Mane's face, but he shook it off as if it caused no effect. Mane grabbed Royce to pick him up and squeezed him until he screamed.

Mane roared!

The vibration of the sound was so intense William covered his ears. "Holy fuck!" William yelled out.

Royce didn't have the strength to cover his ears but tried to open his eyes to the sound as he was being crushed, but Mane dropped him and kicked him toward William's feet. William looked down and saw blood dripping out of Royce's ear.

"Can you still fight, kid?" William asked, trying to pick him up.

"What?" Royce finally grabbed his ears to take cover from the sound but didn't realize they were bleeding. William sighed, realizing he can't hear him.

William helped him up.

"At this rate, we're both gonna die," William said.

"What?"

Mane let out another roar, but not as loud, when a teleportal opened up, and Cin popped through with his hands in his pockets.

"Who are you?" Mane said, stunned he came in from the sky. Cin appeared closer to Mane.

"Well, I've seen enough."

"What?" Mane said with confusion.

Cin's body started to smoke. He pulled his hands out of his pockets and snapped his fingers. Mane caught on a large blazing fire. He screamed as he burned alive, roaring over and over again. The men who were left got onto the motorcycles and drove off, but Cin snapped his fingers again, setting the tires ablaze. The engines on the bike started to blow up one by one, and some simultaneously. They all screamed as they burned alive.

William walked to his vehicle to grab his jacket and tie, glad it was over. "You're welcome," Royce said sarcastically as he watched William walk away. Cin stayed in his position, staring at his brother.

"We really needed the help," Royce admitted. "How long have you been watching before you could help?"

"Long enough to know that you both were going to lose," Cin responded sarcastically. Royce walked past Mane's dead body when one of the motorcycles started smoking again. "Royce!" Cin yelled out. Royce was also catching fire.

"Come on, that shit doesn't work on me," Royce laughed it off.

"Yeah, I know," Cin confirmed his joke while he let out a closed smile.

"Okay, then, I'm out. We can play your games later!" Royce joked back as he walked back to the car.

"I still owe you for the lucky hit you got off of me!" Cin was happy to play back.

"Are you serious? You are so powerful sometimes I forget you're only thirteen," Royce said with a smile.

"Fuck you, Royce!"

Cin snapped his fingers and ignited a fire. The gas tank from Mane's bike blew up into pieces near Royce, sending him forward, flying through the windshield and landing on the top of his hood. Royce tried to look up but then passed out.

Cin felt satisfied and teleported out, then a shadow stood over Royce.

*****

Royce woke up in his bedroom. It was dark. He looked around to collect where he was when he saw a dark figure in the corner.

"Hello? Who's there?" he asked with a stern voice.

The figures stepped into the moonlight coming through the window.

"Angelica? Her figure started to clear. "What the hell are you doing here? How did you get in here?" Royce started to look around again, realizing he didn't have a shirt on. "Where the hell is my shirt?"

"I brought you home after your fight. I took it off because I wanted to see how fast you heal," Angelica explained in a soft tone.

Royce became annoyed. "Well, thanks, but creeper mode isn't necessary."

Angelica moved forward to put her face in the light, causing her fangs to sparkle. Royce flinched at the sight of them.

"Angelica, I don't know what's wrong with you lately, but you need to try to relax."

Angelica said nothing with some heavy breathing, suddenly streaking across the room to jump and bite Royce on the neck.

Royce yelled out with a low vibrating scream, throwing her into the dresser/mirror, slashing it and breaking it into pieces. Angelica stood back up, hissing with her fangs out.

"What the fuck is your problem?" Royce tried to negotiate and backed off the bed. Royce grabbed his neck to look at the blood on his hand.

"I have to taste the blood of the man that was able to kill the leader of the vamps. My husband and the elder, aka my father," Angelica said, snapping back up from the top of the dresser, wiping off the glass on her clothes.

Royce looked down, watching the specks of glass hit the floor. "What the hell are you talking about?" Royce asked with confusion and some fear.

Angelica then glided to him unexpectedly again, biting on the other side of his neck. Royce pushed her through the closet door, breaking it in half. She growled with her teeth out.

"Ward asked me to find the new player."

Royce didn't know what to do, so he didn't move.

"Your first appearance was when you killed my husband, then your blood when you fell on your truck," Angelica hissed to explain, licking blood off her teeth.

Royce still decided to stay silent and not make a move. Angelica looked at him up and down and started to take off her clothes. Royce's eyes widened. Her body was lean and strong with perfect breasts. He froze. Angelica streaked across the room and ripped off his pants before he could stop her.

"I had help. Zinda's portal and Van's satellite," Royce started to explain.

Angelica proceeded to tackle him on the bed, making it clear she wanted to have sex. She bit Royce on the shoulder. He screamed and got up, holding her on top, but she didn't let go as he slammed her into anything he had the strength to reach. No matter how hard he resisted, he inserted himself inside of her. Angelica thrust forward to make it penetrate. They became in heat and thrust back and forth against the wall until he was done.

Royce was out of breath and threw himself on the bed. Angelica's energy was now calm as she was putting her clothes back on. Royce was laying there with some blood and bruising but was starting to heal. Angelica stared, fascinated by this so-called normal who is obviously not.

"What are you doing?" Royce asked her, catching his breath. "The sun will be coming up soon, and I'm not a cuddler."

"When do you want to do this again? Royce asked, not knowing if he was turned on or in fear.

"I'll let you know when I need to," Angelica said, biting her bottom lip, showing the tip of her fang.

"You don't have to be so cold about it," Royce said, disappointed.

"Well, I'm a vamp, how else?"

Angelica streaked out the window in a flash.

"Crazy cold-blooded bitch," Royce said as he banged his head against the pillow to pass out.

When Royce awoke, Van was standing over him. "Royce, wake up! What the hell happened?" Everything in his room was damaged.

"Van? How did you get in?"

"You must be out of it if you think a locked door can stop me from getting anywhere?"

"I see your point. Still creepy. I could have had a woman in here, you know."

Van pointed to his holoscreen. "Get up and get dressed. It's time to go to work. Your truck is done, but when Gears gets out of school, he wants to talk to you about the squad car."

Royce had no idea what he was talking about and jerked his eyebrows together. "I really don't care what that little smug shit has to say."

"Let's just go," Van instructed.

"Wait, school? He's in school?" Royce asked. "Yes, he's twelve," Van said sarcastically.

Outside of a beautiful red brick building was a school, New Jericho Academy. The trees were abundant, and the grass was shimmering green with white flowers lingering in spots. Gears was sitting against the largest tree in the yard with other kids walking around the grounds.

A girl carrying some books in a cute pink summer dress walked over to him. He looked up to see a pretty girl as her long hair flared in the wind.

"Hello, Eva!" Gears said with excitement.

"Hey, Gears, how are you doing?" the young, sweet-toned girl turned to look at him, replying with a smile.

"Better now," he directed as he stared into her eyes.

"What are you reading?" she asked.

"Theory on Hoover vehicles." He tried to show her the book.

"Can you walk me to class? she asked with a smile.

He grabbed his books to get up while he tried to grab hers.

Gears suddenly tripped and dropped everything. Eva tried to help, but a shadow came over. When Gears looked up, Cin was standing over him.

"You should be more careful carrying my girl's books." Cin smiled.

Gears didn't say a word, fearful, and handed Eva back her books, trying to clean the grass off and retrieving his.

"Well?" Cin said, stepping closer to Gears's face.

"Are you bullying me because I'm walking with the girl that you like? I mean, you can't be serious? You've seen too many movies, Cin."

Cin suddenly punched him in the stomach.

"Cin! I'm going to get a teacher if you don't stop," Eva yelled out.

"No, just get to class before you're late," Cin instructed her.

Gears was on the ground, trying to catch his breath.

"Besides, you can do better than this goofy ass...boy," Cin told Eva with a condescending tone.

"You may be thirteen, but you act five," Gears said as he tried to stand back up. Cin looked back at Gears to push him to the ground.

"No!" Eva yelled again, not knowing what to do.

"Go, Eva, just go!" Gears yelled at Eva.

Eva ran off with a disappointed look on her face.

Cin tried to follow her when Gears ran off to the corner of the building and looked back, but Cin wasn't following.

The kids around just ignored the bell as it started to ring. Gears took a deep breath, thinking it was over when he looked forward, but Cin was standing in front of him.

"So you want to try to embarrass me in front of Eva?"

"You embarrassed yourself. You don't need me for that."

"You don't know when to shut up, do you?"

"No, because I know you like to hear yourself talk."

Cin punched Gears in the stomach, and he fell to his knees for a second time. Gears tried to punch him back, but Cin teleported behind him and pushed him to the ground with his foot. Gears was on the ground, barely breathing. Cin walked away.

Embarrassed, Gears grabbed his stuff and limped to the bus station to head back to the precinct.

*****

Gears arrived at the shop in the precinct and headed straight to the bathroom. He examined his bruising in the mirror and flinches with anger. "All right, Cin, you teleporting motherfucker. I'll show you that you are not special," Gears said out loud.

He then heard footsteps. Van and Royce walked into the shop, noticing Gears's book bag on the chair.

"Gears! Are you here?" Van called out.

"Yeah! Coming."

Gears covered up his chest before he walked out into the open but grabbed his bag of ice to cover up his eye. "I thought you were in school?"

"Damn what the hell happened to you?" Royce asked.

"Why are you here?" Gears asked, annoyed.

"My baby, why else?"

"What the hell is your problem, Royce? How the hell do you destroy every single car you get? You're making my job that much harder."

"Just do your job, kid, and don't worry about it."

This angered Gears, and he grabbed a hammer sitting on the side of a table.

"Hey! Hold on," Van yelled.

"It's not my fault you got your ass beat today," Royce recanted.

Gear put the hammer down with a big sigh. "I need a fucking break."

Van looked at Gears with empathy. "Hey, I understand, but we still have a lot of work to do. We all get it from time to time," Van explained, grabbing Gears's shoulders.

"I just feel like I'm doing all of your guys' work. I've never seen such a helpless group of adults before," Gears said in his immature tone.

"Okay, I'll talk to Ward for you about our project. Calm down," Van said while Royce was in the background acting like an asshole, rolling his eyes.

Royce and Van got in his truck to pull out, but Royce rolled down his window to yell out, "Hey! Whoever did that to you, get his ass." Royce winked as he waved him off.

"Just leave," Gears said under his breath.

"So where to first?" Van asked.

"We need to get to Philario and get him out of his deal," Royce encouraged.

"With Cin?"

"Yeah."

"We need to talk about all this, Royce. If we're going to work together, we need to talk to each other. One of us is going to die if you keep shit to yourself."

"Well, let's go get some ink, and I will explain on the way." Royce decided to comply.

"Ink?"

"Yeah, ink." Royce didn't explain.

Royce took a U-turn and headed to Radd's Accessories.

CHAPTER 8

The Reset

B ack at the precinct, Ward walked into the auto shop. Gears was
working on some glasses with a tiny device that was creating
blue and red sparks that faded quickly.

"Hey, Gears, what you working on?"

"Revenge," Gears offered a short answer and followed up with
"What can I do for you?"

Ward took a deep sigh and slouched on the table next to him
to take a seat. "I can feel your frustration all over the precinct.
Something we can talk about?"

"Yes, I know. I just need a break. I'm going to take a break after mine and Van's next project. I can't work with NJPD right now," Gears said while still working on his glasses.

"Listen, not a problem. Just let me know if you need anything," Ward said, and he got up to touch Gears's shoulder as he walked out.

Gears slightly turned back around, removing his goggles, to watch him walk away, but then decided to say, "I know I still owe you for taking care of me. You saved me from the vamps that killed my parents. I will never forget that."

"You don't owe me anything. Not only are you a son to me, but the whole NJPD thinks of you as their son. Well, except Royce. But just look at him as your annoying older brother," Ward joked. "One last thing. Do you need help with your face?" Ward offered with a wink. Gears shook his head no. Ward returned a nod and left the shop.

Gears put his goggles back on and continued working.

*****

Royce and Van arrived at Radd's.

Van had never been there before and started to look around. "What is this place? It looks like a pawnshop or antique shop. Or is this the tattoo shop?" Van asked as he continued to investigate the old building.

Before they could walk in, Radd came out to greet them. "Well, how have you been, son?" Radd asked Royce.

"Good, and you, old man?" Royce answered with a smile and then pointed to Van. "This is my partner."

Radd nodded his head. "Nice to meet you, man. What brings you guys in?"

"We've been in a couple of fights, and I think there's something that you can help me with." Radd was pleased to see Royce was starting to take him down as his mentor.

"This sounds good. Come in and sit down. Tell me."

Van was surprised by all the weapons on the walls and devices of different gadgets, ink, and stones he couldn't explain. But he smiled and sat without asking any questions.

"I've been fighting a teleporter, a fire starter, and a werelion," Royce explained.

"A werelion? Wow, really?" Radd said with a surprised look.

Van was listening and realized there were fights he wasn't aware of. "You've been busy, Royce," Van interrupted.

"Yes, there's a lot that goes on in this city. Especially some stuff that NJPD doesn't know about," Radd explained to Van.

"Like what else? Royce asked.

"Do you trust him?" Radd said in a serious tone and crossed his fingers. "Yes, he's my partner."

"The reset. Tell me about that," Royce asked.

"Oh, I didn't realize we'd be getting that serious so soon. I don't think you're ready for this information, but okay, son. Every five hundred years, the world resets," Radd started to explain.

"What? What the hell are you talking about?" Royce interrupted.

Radd put his hands up to gesture to them to come with him. "Wait, follow me. Let me keep going, and I'll explain."

Van and Royce reached the roof with Radd leading. They both were speculative but decided to listen.

"You think this is the only city on this planet? Well, that's not true. There's actually seven cities within," Radd said, trying not to shock them.

"Are you saying that we've been lied to all this time?" Van asked.

"Not necessarily. Most people don't know that there are other cities. In fact, 99% of people don't know. Including some people that are in NJPD, I'm sure."

"What, no way. Ward?" Van stated with frustration but continued. "This is bullshit. There can't be," Van insisted.

"Shut up then. Let him finish," Royce argued with a soft tone.

"Each city has a different type of technology. There are different demons at each center of each one. There are predominate races in each one, just like here. Their abilities are also going to be different."

Van couldn't hold his breath any longer. "So V is a demon?" Van started to realize that some of this started to make sense.

"Yes, he's not just the richest and most powerful man in the city. He also runs everything. Even your dad," Radd noted as he looked at Royce.

Royce made no expression, but he then pointed to the skyscraper in the center of the city.

"New Jericho is the center of all the cities," Radd explained.

"And what is the reset?" Royce asked.

"Six demons and their leader can reset all the cities when a cycle passes. So no one person or group gets too powerful to overthrow them. BUT each generation does get stronger though."

Van and Royce both were contemplating on the information when Radd was done talking on the roof. "Let's get back down."

They followed Radd back inside, and Royce took his shirt off and sat in the tattoo chair. "This is crazy. But is there anything we can do?" Van asked, concerned, confused.

"You're going to have to kill V," Radd said.

"A demon from another city?" Royce said with discouragement.

"It might postpone the reset. But V is the key. So back to what you were saying earlier. The teleporter and fire starter."

"The lion had insane strength and ability," Royce told Radd.

"I know, so let's fix you up," Radd said, walking over to the tattoo chair.

Van watched closely. "All right, explain the tattoo. They give you powers?" Van initiated.

"No, these tattoos will amplify what powers are already within you," Radd explained and then turned back to Royce. "I will put this owl head on your upper back or lower neck, and it will heighten your senses. Lastly, an anvil on your back for strength."

Radd started to prepare the ink.

"Good, I owe Tank round two!" Royce said like a loaded warrior.

"Tank?" Radd said with a smirk. "You'll never be as strong as Tank. This amplifies your natural strength, but his is greater than yours. So his tat has a greater effect. You will need multiple strength tats to get there, and it won't be today. There's no way your body could take that much."

Van was impressed. "Can anyone get these?"

"Yes, but I decide who. And I will be out of ink after this," Radd said sarcastically.

"I didn't want one, anyway," Van said with a nonchalant tone, getting up, looking around the room, ready to go.

"I will need two days with you for training," Radd requested.

"I'm good with that. Van, can you cover me for those two days?" Royce asked.

"I think I'm going to need two days to process this event," Van agreed sarcastically.

"All right, here's my keys, but please be careful," Royce said, handing them over.

"Nah, I'm good. You keep them. I can get places faster than that truck," Van said sarcastically. Van headed out of the shop as Radd started pressing on the needle and defining the first tattoo.

When Van got outside, he saw police lights a few blocks away. He started walking toward the lights. He saw a black SUV that hit a pole. Zinda was in the middle of the street.

There was a large purple haze, and her eyes were glowing. Angelica wasn't standing far from her. "What's going on? What is Zinda doing?" Van walked toward Angelica.

"Triple murder," Zinda was speaking but in a spell to see the event.

"Both men were shot from the rooftop across the street," she again started to explain.

"And the third?" Van asked.

"Stabbed in the heart with a weird blade." Van's eyes widened.

"Was this on the rooftop?" Zinda pointed.

"Take us there now!" Van ordered.

Zinda lifted both of her hands, and a purple haze wrapped around them when they appeared on the rooftop.

Van pulled up his holoscreen.

"You guys get those bodies to NJPD!" Van yelled out.

"Van, what's wrong?" Angelica asked, looking confused.

"Like I said, get them to the NJPD now! I need the bullets removed and the blade designed," he ordered the girls.

Van rushed out in a flash back to the NJPD. Once he arrived, he went straight to the auto shop, and Gears was working on that same device.

"Gears, what are you doing here? Don't you have school tomorrow?"

"Yeah, I had to finish this up. I'm leaving now."

Gears put on those glasses which had a heavy red tint, then left. Van didn't have time to listen to the last of his sentence and headed to Ward's office.

"What are you still doing here?" Ward asked Van.

"There were three bodies earlier. I'm checking in on them. Did you get all the information from Zinda and Angelica?"

"Yes, I heard about it. Do you think it's him?" Ward asked.

"I don't know, but that's why I came back right away. I had figured the report would be done by the time I got back." Ward handed Van the report and the bag of bullets that were in it.

"He's back, but I need you to stay focused. Because the last time, he almost killed both of you guys," Ward confirmed what Van was thinking.

"He will die this time," Van debated.

"Listen, I want you to wait until morning. I'm assuming Royce went home. You two get on it first thing. You will need his help on this one," Ward ordered.

Van walked out, passing Milo and Buster goofing off.

"Milo, Buster," Van said, stopping in his tracks.

"Hey, man, our shift is over, and we're not trying to hear it," Milo said sarcastically.

"Listen, he's back. I'm going to need all the hands I can get," Van explained.

Milo and Buster both stopped playing.

"Okay, tomorrow will push some people around," Buster said in a serious tone as he pumped his fist in his other hand with Milo.

Right then, Zinda and Angelica walked into the precinct again.

"Hey, Zinda, Angelica, your number one priority is to get me the info on the murders from earlier. I'm going to get some more answers soon," Van instructed.

*****

A little later that evening, Van is standing outside of a run-down club. The scene was made of trashy-looking people, and there were two werewolf bouncers standing by the door. Van tried to walk in, but the werewolves stood in front of him, not letting him pass.

"No NJPD allowed up in here," the first werewolf grunted.

Van took his badge out of his pocket and gave it to the bouncer, then quickly walked in between them. Both of them growled.

Van walked in on a bunch of normals with male and female ogres. A huge glass tank laid out one side of the wall with two mermaids with glowing fishtails. Everyone, including the mermaids, stopped when he walked in and noticed. Some were disgusted and got up to leave.

Van looked around to yell, "I'm looking for any info about three men killed today in the street."

A man yelled in return, "We don't talk to cops!"

Van turned to look at the man who yelled out, "I'm not asking as a cop. This is personal. I don't even have my badge." He then opened his coat to prove he gave up his badge.

The crowd still looked evasive or disgusted by his presence. But Van didn't budge. A man approached Van with a pool cue and tried to swing at Van. But he caught it and took it from him, hitting the man across the face. The cue broke in half, sending the man over the pool table. Another man rushed Van from behind and tried to kick him, but he turned to catch his leg and stabbed him with the broken cue.

Everyone stood up, defensive. The bouncers walked when they heard the commotion. Van looked around at the two werewolves that were walking toward him.

"This is your last chance," Van said, standing firm.

"Yes, your last chance to pray!" one of the ogres yelled out.

"Fine, everybody dies!" Van said playfully and pulled up his holoscreen, but before Van could push the button, a purple mist filled the room with Zinda and Angelica appearing. Zinda raised her hands to create a purple shock wave, pinning everyone against the wall. She held her hands up, waiting for Van's instruction, but when he didn't say anything, Zinda strongly suggested with her eyes fixated in the air, "Let's go, we're leaving."

"Wait," Angelica told Zinda. She pulled her gun and changed the magazine and walked over to the two women on the wall and, without warning, shot both of them in the head. Light came out of their eyes, mouth, ears, and they screamed as they melted into pieces. "Okay, now we can go," Angelica stated, putting away her weapon.

Van smiled and walked to the werewolf bouncers, grabbing his badge back. "Thanks!"

Purple mist filled the room as Angelica, Van, and Zinda disappeared. The smoke and purple haze dropped, and everyone dropped to the floor, barely breathing.

*****

Zinda, Van, and Angelica appeared in front of the precinct closely together, then slightly walked apart.

"Go home, or I'll report that you were about to kill everybody in the club," Zinda said with force, upset with Van.

Van looked with his eyes batting as if he didn't really care, but he would rather not argue and nodded his head yes.

"Before you go, have you seen Royce?" Angelica asked.

Van stared at Angelica but was too frustrated to answer. He slowly walked off.

The next morning, in the courtyard of the New Jericho Academy, Gears was sitting at his usual tree when Eva walked up.

"Hello, Gears," Eva said, not knowing if he was mad at her. When he looked, she saw the bruises and lump on his face.

"Oh, Gears, I'm so sorry. Is there anything I can do?" Eva asked.

"Yes, stay with me. Cin will probably show up soon." He hoped she would agree.

"Please don't fight him again. I don't want to see you hurt," Eva pleaded with him when Cin walked up.

"Then leave, Eva." Gears realized she didn't need to see the violence when he saw Cin clenching his fist.

Eva ran off as Gears puts on his red-tinted glasses.

"So you didn't learn your lesson yesterday?" Cin said, staring at Gears. "You're such a genius, aren't you, with those glasses."

"You know how stupid you are? Eva would never go for you, Cin."

"She's already mine, Gears. She just doesn't know it." Cin got closer to Gears's face and put his finger on his right shoulder, pushing him back.

Gears didn't say anything or push back.

Cin punched Gears in the face, and he fell to the ground, but the glasses stayed in place as he designed them to. Kids started to surround them on the grassy knoll. Cin then teleported to kick Gears while he was down, but there was a red flash, and he moved out of the way. He was wearing a ring device that turned into a brass knuckle, and he punched Cin in the nuts. Cin screamed and fell to his knees in pain, grunting and holding onto his abdominal area. Cin was about to snap his fingers, but someone grabbed his hand. He looked up and saw a teacher with Eva standing there.

"Everyone back to class now!" the teacher yelled and directed everybody in toward the doors with his finger in anger.

As the crowd departed, Cin stood up, shocked that Gears could fight back. But the teacher yanked him forward to go inside the building.

"How did you do that? How did you hit him like that?" Eva asked, blushing.

"I made these glasses that detect dimension distortion. But it takes up so much power, and it only works once, then it needs to be charged. I'm going to have to optimize it somehow. But I figured I could at least get one good hit," Gears said and giggled with her.

Eva smiled even more, looking him directly in the eyes as she batted her eyelashes. "You're amazing," she said, a little giddy.

"Thanks. So have you seen the new *Vampire Hunter* cartoon?"

"No, tell me about it," Eva said as she hugged her books.

Gears grabbed them from her and held her hand with the other to walk her to class.

*****

Van rushed over to Radd's shop and knocked to see if anyone was there. "Hey, Van," Radd answered the door. "Finally process everything?"

"Listen, I need help with a case," Van told Radd, looking around for Royce.

"I told you I needed two days," Radd recanted.

Van shook his head. "I can't. It's important."

"More important than the reset?" Radd suggested.

"I don't know what to believe anymore, but we have to go."

"I'll go ask Royce. I'll be right back. Wait here."

Radd disappeared behind the curtain to enter an elevator that had one button to close the doors, elevating downward. Van could hear the doors compress when they came back to the top.

Royce emerged from the curtain. "You ready?"

"Let's go," Van agreed.

"Only if we go see V. I'm sure your case is important, but we have to look into this reset shit too."

Van sighed. "Let's do it."

CHAPTER 9

The Trinity

William was looking at some blueprints that were laid out over his desk when he sensed Cin from behind. "What is it, Cin?"

"You always know when I teleport in," Cin said with disappointment.

"Why are you not in school?"

"I got suspended," Cin answered.

"Aw, yes, I heard. He got half a hit off of you too, huh? A scrawny kid like that?" William said, disappointed.

"That guy's a fucking genius! He made glasses that can see my every move," Cin said with frustration.

"Excuses, excuses. Sometimes I wonder if I picked the wrong son," William said in a condescending tone.

Cin teleported away in anger, appearing at the top of V's tower. The sky was orange, yellow, and blue with a clean scent in the air. He walked over to a gargoyle to the right of him, looking out into the sky. He sat down near it. He sighed as he pulled a button out of his pocket, pushing it while leaning back, and fell asleep.

*****

In a building on the first floor, Royce and Van walked into V's lobby, which was completely empty. "Hello?" Royce echoed through the hall.

"This is weird, but let's head up."

They took the elevator to the top floor. The door opened, and they looked around, still dumbfounded by the silence. They looked around and saw the whole floor was a beautiful wooded area.

"What the hell?" Royce said.

"It's beautiful," Van said with a glaze in his eye.

When they finally snapped back from their amazement, two curved white desks were there sheltering two women with a huge mirrored door behind them. As they reached the door a five-foot-five Asian woman with short black hair, wearing a white pantsuit, stepped out in front of them as if she just appeared out of nowhere.

"Hello, Detectives, my name is Toxis. Can I help you?" she asked.

"We're here to see V." Royce stated with a straight face, trying not to look at her up and down.

"That will be Victor to you," Toxis proclaimed.

"Whatever, tell him we need to see him," Royce said again.

Another woman stood up and stepped toward the front door. She stood at six feet and four inches, had long black hair, was White, and was in an enduring white leather spandex suit on.

"Holy shit!" Van said.

"Hello, my name is Talan, and if you don't have an appointment, you're going to have to leave now," she said in a demanding, straightforward voice with no expression on her face.

"Van, why is this bitch eyeballing me?" Royce asked in a sarcastic tone.

Talan became angry and balled her fists as Toxis reached for her gun, but the mirror doors opened from behind them. The women stepped aside in military style as Royce and Van walked in. Royce almost stuck his tongue out to the woman, and Van shook his head no.

A six-foot White man with short blond hair, wearing a white suit, stood behind a marble desk. A gorgeous Black woman stood next to him who was five feet eight, with curly short hair, wearing a white sundress, which Royce noticed.

"V, I'm assuming?" Van asked.

"It's Victor to you," Toxis repeated.

"It's fine, they're NJPD. They keep our city safe. We're going to be courteous to them. And they can call me V. Sorry my assistants are so aggressive. The little one behind you is Toxis, and the big one, well, be careful, she's an Amazon."

"Bullshit, Amazons are a myth," Van said as he stared at her.

"Oh, come on, you guys are not that closed-minded, are you? What did you need me to teach you today?" V asked with sarcasm.

"Ah, the reset?" Royce asked sarcastically.

Everybody turned to look at Royce with an intense stare. Even Van wanted to ease into it and looked at Royce with rotating eyes.

"The last girl that you haven't met is Tifini," V stated to finish his introductions as he felt he should not be interrupted.

"Don't dodge, it looks weak," Royce demanded when suddenly, the whole room started to shake, and leaves fell from the trees from the outside view of the office. V became angry. "Everyone is on command. The whole city takes orders from me!" he stated.

The shaking was getting unbearable.

"Sir!" Tifini yelled to direct him to calm down as she almost fell down. V allowed the shaking to come to a halt.

"Just tell me why you are here, Detectives," V asked in a professional manner.

"To see if what we heard was true," Van explained.

"I think we have our answer," Royce commented. V nodded and sat down, waiting for them to leave. Royce and Van took the hint.

Van and Royce walked past the trinity before they entered the elevator. They all stared at each other as their doors were closing. V instructed the ladies to "make sure that our new friends get home safe."

When they finally reached the truck, William walked up. "What the hell are you guys doing, Royce?" William asked.

"What the hell do you want? We're working," Royce answered with sarcasm and anger.

"I don't know what the hell you're doing here, but you are on his radar now. If you piss him off, which I'm sure you did, he will send the girls after you, and they never miss. They have an Amazon on their side."

"Scared, old man?" Royce said.

"The last time she and I had words, she almost snapped my neck, and she would have if V didn't stop her. I remember that you barely beat me the last time, Royce. You don't have the strength to beat her," William said in a fatherly tone.

Royce ended the conversation with William by getting into the vehicle.

*****

Cin was still lingering on the building, sleeping. A purple haze started to flourish around him. A man appeared who was White, five feet seven, with purple tennis shoes, black pants, black hoodie with the hood up, long hair hanging over his face, and glowing purple eyes.

"Good to see you, Cin. Where is Denia?" he asked.

"I'm here, Cin," Denia yelled.

Cin looked around and saw no one. Then suddenly, a Hispanic woman appeared. She was about five-foot-seven, wearing white tennis shoes, tight black long-sleeved shirt, and a white tennis skirt. Her hair was long and brown, but it was in a ponytail, very thick-looking, that dangled to her shoulders. She had about three knives strapped to both thighs and a short sword strapped to the small of her back.

"You get me with that every time," Cin said.

They all appeared to glance but then became silent to watch the sunset set in. The gargoyle next to them came to life, grunted, and yelped out as he stretched the molding pieces off of him. He was very tall once he stretched his limbs all the way, six feet eight in height with skin made of gray stone.

"Good morning, Ivor," Cin welcomed. Ivor grunted but didn't reply.

"So is V not keeping his word?" Denia asked Cin.

"Feels good to have 'the heathens' together. It's time we secure our position in this reset," Cin said, looking at his team.

Oh, what a big surprise," Zindo answered, not waiting on Cin's.

*****

As Royce and Van approached the downtown area, not much seemed to be happening. It was somewhat dim and foggy even though the sun was out. They were both quiet as Van was navigating the GPS from the car screen. Royce looked at Van and sighed. "So do you believe all of this?" he asked, but Van was barely paying attention.

"I don't know what to believe. However, we need to decide whether we're going to tell the department to figure out what is next."

"Yes, we have to," Royce indirectly agreed. "We're going to need all the help we can get," Royce continued, staring out the windshield, resting his head on his hand with his arm against the door window.

"Listen, he owns the city, Royce, and there's no telling what or who he has under his thumb. But maybe we need to break down his empire first, figure out who he's connected to. And maybe we should go back and talk to Radd. He probably knows more than we do."

"Hell yeah, now that's what I'm talking about." Royce was excited that Van was starting to warm up to Radd.

Van cracked a smile as Royce was ready to take a left at the corner when gunfire hit the front of Royce's truck. He immediately swung it to the right, and they covered themselves as best they could with their gear. Royce slammed brakes as people were running for cover to avoid hitting a building.

"Holy shit!" Royce yelled out. But nothing was able to get through the windows on the truck. Van and Royce realized that Gears must have armored the truck with a bulletproof shield throughout the entire material. "This kid's a fucking genius!" Royce yelled out with excitement. They looked through the windshield and saw Toxis standing in the middle of the street. She was holding a machine gun with Talan and Tifini standing behind her.

"Let's go," Van instructed as Royce signaled yes.

Van and Royce got out of the truck but took cover behind the doors. They were not standing far from them when Tifini yelled out, "Hello again, Detectives! We need to talk." Van was about to reply when Toxis continued with gunfire.

Royce and Van cringed down waiting for it to stop.

"I thought you said let's talk?" Royce yelled out, looking around to see if more gunfire was about to flare.

"We are talking! Can't you hear? Tifini responded.

"Loud and clear now!" Van responded with sarcasm.

Van and Royce were still taking cover and still were not in their view. Toxis looked up at the rooftop to point to the others. Talan and Tifini locked fingers as she pressed her foot against her hand to leap up and launch her on the three-story building. She then proceeded to pull two spheres out of her pocket and tossed them into the air. They sprouted small chrome propellers and hovered.

Van and Royce were still peeking out on the sides of the truck but with the blockage to examine the area, trying to locate where they are.

"Van turned to Royce. "Where is Toxis?"

"How am I supposed to know?"

"You're not watching?"

"No, I thought you were," Van whispered over to Royce with a sarcastic tone.

They were both holding their guns against their chest, feeling their life on the line. "Why don't you use your satellite, Mr. Holoscreen?" Royce stated with frustration.

"What do you think I'm trying to do over here?" Van started pressing buttons, but only static was coming from his wrist. "They are blocking me somehow. The whole city is blocked by the static, and it's interfering with my connection," Van stated.

Royce took a chance and shot back, but he got rained down by bullets attacking him. He retracted, taking cover.

"They are coordinated!" Van said with a sarcastic laugh because Royce looked scared.

The level of disrespect you showed V will not go unchecked!" Talan yelled out.

"Damn, that warrants death?" Van yelled out to be comedic.

Royce rolled his eyes. "Seriously? You're going to try to play right now?" he said while staring at Van. Van smiled back, shrugging his shoulders.

"Well, we're not here to make friendships," Talan said sarcastically.

Van tried to run or attempted to run from one car to another, attempting a better angle, but he was blocked by the gunfire again.

"You're gonna have to take Toxis out first," Royce insisted with a smirk.

"Can you take Tifini and Talan on by yourself, or hold them back?"

"Are you kidding me? It's just two girls," Royce said sarcastically but then looked serious.

Van took a deep sigh, "Wait until Talan and Tifini get close. That way Toxis will stop shooting. Then I'll be able to go. Don't forget Talan might be an Amazon. She's not an easy kill," Van warned Royce.

"Okay. Amazon. Got it." Royce had no clue what the fuck he was in for.

Talan walked to Van's side of the truck slowly as Tifini walked over to Royce's. Royce got up from his side, jumping over the hood to kick Talan in the chest, knocking her to the ground. Van ran to the closet alleyway while bullets ricocheted off the ground behind him, not being able to catch him. Tifini threw punches and kicked Royce, but he dodged all of them all. He grabbed her by her arm and threw her onto the car parked across the street. She bashed into it and fell into the ground. Talan walked over to Royce. He threw a punch, but she caught it, then kicked Royce in the chest, sending him flying into the street lamp, slamming him to the ground. Royce was hurt and stayed on the ground, holding his chest.

"Van, she's an Amazon!" Royce yelled, out of breath but loud enough for Van to hear.

Van shook his head while climbing the fire escapes. "I tried to tell you," he whispered under his breath, trying to spot Toxis. His holoscreen was still jammed.

"Damn! How are they doing this crap?" Van said to himself with a heavy, disappointed tone when a tinkling, distinctive sound suddenly trickled near him. When he looked down, he saw a grenade rolling down toward him. His anxious response was an immediate jump off the building to the next roof as it blew everything into pieces, and fire flew through the sky. *Damn, these girls are good. Think, Van, think!*

He started running, letting out a couple of shots from his gun, backward, forward, and sideways. He leaped off the fire escapes and onto other rooftops, taking cover behind a wall. He tried his holoscreen once more, trying to concentrate. It mapped out coordinates finally. He navigated it to allow him a better military angle to take her out. He prevented Talan from attacking Royce along with others by letting out shots where they could see him, allowing him to climb down without them knowing his angle.

Royce used this time to his advantage and started fighting both Talan and Tifini. They were beating each other equally, and blood was gushing everywhere. Royce healed quickly each time and kept moving as they fought in fast motion to keep him off of them.

"I have to admit I'm impressed!" Talan smiled as she was getting off the ground.

"I agree!" Royce yelled out, somewhat out of breath.

Tifini came to defend her. "Tifini, stay back until I give you a signal!" Talan yelled out.

Royce and Talan faced off, quickly landing punches to each other's face. Major shock waves rambled through the ground and on air. They intensely hit back and forth, which crashed in some of the building's windows from the waves of the blows. Royce stumbles as Talan punched him in the stomach unexpectedly with one of her hits. But it didn't take him down. Royce grabbed her arm and threw her onto a car, landing on the hood. He took that moment to jump and landed on her stomach as he held his body weight on her. A shock wave rattled the vehicle, breaking the cement beneath. Talan coughed up blood that splattered on her jumpsuit. Talan looked out for the count, so Royce jumped down while wiping blood from his nose and mouth.

Tifini ran toward him from a distance to help her.

"Come on! You guys fight like girls. Even like this, you can't beat me!" Royce yelled at her as Tifini's face was melted in anger and determination.

They both had the same amount of strength against each other as the fight dragged on, creating a visible pain and anger on their faces. She finally was able to grip his leg across hers and punched but missed. But she took a deep breath and headbutted him in the head. Royce hesitated to punch back and then lost his balance. Tifini took this advantage when he landed on the ground, and kicked him, sending him sliding across it.

Van was back on another roof, trying to find a good spot. More grenades were landing near him. He searched for fire escapes quickly to climb. Five more explosions happened all at the same time.

He ran but got caught in the vibration of the explosion, throwing him off the roof. He landed hard, hitting his head on the fire escape on the next building, but was able to pull himself up right quickly. He punched his gear for the holoscreen, and it pulled up with a beaming red light. It picked up another coordinate.

"That should do it," Van said with a sigh of relief to himself.

Van passed out as a small beam came down from the sky and went through Toxis's arm and leg as she screamed.

Royce rose to his knees, bloody, kneeling in front of Tifini as Talan walked up and punched Royce in the face, sending him back to the ground. And with an extensive stretch of her leg, she kicked him, sending him through a bus stop bench ten feet away. It cracked in half, and pieces of the bench landed on top of him. Talan, who was slightly limping, walked toward his direction, wanting to finish him.

Toxis came toward them, limping.

"We need to leave now! I don't know if Van is coming!" The other girls looked at Talan, surprised because she looked beaten.

"Are you okay?" Tifini looked worried.

"I can't continue. My arm is broke, and a couple ribs, I think," Talan said with pain in her voice.

"We need to go! They're going to have backup coming soon, and we need to retreat!" Toxis yelled out again.

Suddenly you could hear the NJPD sirens and lights coming toward them. Loud and clear. "Let's go!" Tifini yelled out.

Royce pushed most of the debris off him, including the large piece of bench, trying to stand.

"Oh, you got to be kidding me. What is he?" Talan muttered, watching Royce right before Tifini put the palm of her hand on the ground, and they fell through a portal.

Royce's eyes widened. "Well, that's convenient."

When the NJPD rushed in, they headed over to help Royce. "Don't worry about me, find Van. He's probably still on the rooftop." Everybody looked up toward the sky, trying to figure out which rooftop they should search first.

Zinda appeared next to Royce with a purple mist. "No, don't move anyone. It's okay. Angelica found Van, and she took him to the hospital. He's fine," Zinda instructed.

"How did you find him so fast?" Royce asked.

"He was bleeding, but like I said, he was fine," Zinda answered.

"I want to go there. Now," Royce demanded.

Royce walked slowly over to his truck, and Angelica was waiting for him in the passenger's seat.

"Well, you smell amazing." Angelica sniffed Royce's blood all over his clothes, and he was still bleeding. She looked over, and her fangs emerged quickly as she bit his neck.

Royce pushed her off, pulling out his gun in her direction. Angelica hissed with her tongue, rubbing against her teeth.

"What the fuck is your problem? Get the fuck out of my truck, and go do your job."

"You are denying me now?" Angelica said as if she didn't just rip a piece of his neck off. Royce pulled the hammer back, instructing Angelica to get out. Royce didn't look back as she stared at him driving off.

Zinda spotted Angelica by Royce's truck, watching him leave, and heads over to pry. "Everything okay?" she asked, but Angelica was still in a daze.

"Hey, Angelica, explanation!" Zinda voiced to get her attention.

"Are you good? Can I go?" Angelica asked, ignoring her comment.

"Yeah, but you need to help me first," Zinda said with some confusion toward her disconnect. "How many were fighting here?"

"I can smell five. Royce, Van, and three more," Angelica responded but without looking at her.

Zinda nodded her head and walked toward the others investigating the scene. Angelica streaked away.

CHAPTER 10

V

Royce walked in a rush when he arrived at NJ City Hospital. He asked the clerk to lead him to Van.

"Next floor, room 35."

Royce caught the elevator and turned the corner, passing a few nurses that surprisingly didn't get his attention.

"Wassup, man? You doing okay?" Royce asked with genuine concern.

"Aw, you love me," Van responded sarcastically but answered, "My head is just killing me."

A doctor from behind walked in to interrupt. "Van needs his rest. He keeps going in and out of consciousness," the doctor explained. When Royce looked back at Van, he went unconscious.

"And, Detective, by the way, you look like you could use some medical attention too," the doctor said with some concern and sarcasm at the same time.

"Not now, Doc. Can you just leave us alone for a minute?" Royce responded.

The doctor left, shaking his head in disapproval. "You guys will never learn," the doctor mumbled loud enough for Royce to hear.

Van came back too. "Hey, you should be healed by now."

Royce looked at his wounds, grabbed his shoulder that was bleeding on one side to examine it. "I don't know, don't worry about it though. How did you get Toxis? Thought you couldn't see anything."

"I calculated her location by trajectory and the placement of the grenades in three places. So I did get her?"

"Yes, in the arm and leg," Royce confirmed.

"Damn, so after all that I missed," Van rebutted with sadness.

"You're kidding, right?" Van shook his head no. "Well, don't worry about it," Royce retracted. "We'll get them soon enough. You need to get your rest. I'll check in on you tomorrow." Royce tapped Van on his leg to let him know he was leaving.

*****

Back at V's offices, Talan, Tifini, and Toxis are standing in front of his desk. Beaten badly and bandaged.

"Are you fucking serious?" The trinity went after two guys, and not only did you fail, you came back like this?" V asked with anger.

"They are a lot stronger and more prepared than we expected," Toxis tried to argue.

"But we understand how to beat Royce now. Van and the rest of the special unit shouldn't be a problem," Tifini tried to persuade V to still count on them,

"You are missing the point. They will see us coming now. You weren't supposed to fail!" V yelled, sending a thunder through the room as he slammed his fist against his desk.

"Sir, this is the first time we've ever failed a mission," Talan argued in a low voice.

"If you're not 100%, then you are fucking useless!" V said as he turned to look out his window, slamming his hand against the window. A shock wave pushed the girls in the air and banged their backs against the floor, cracking it in several areas around them.

"Get up and get the fuck out!"

*****

Radd got out of his car and looked up at the tall silver-and-black building in front of him. The NJPD Hospital sign seemed to glimmer in the sun. It made him realize things could get worse. He shook himself out of the negative thoughts and decided to pay Van a visit.

"How are you feeling, Van?"

Van was still going in and out of consciousness, but he acknowledged him. "How are you feeling?" Radd repeated.

"Little better," Van responded in a groggy voice.

"Now tell me. It was Talan, Toxis, and Tifini?"

"Yes," Van replied, confused. "How did you know that?"

Radd turned on the TV. A news reporter was still at the crime scene.

"There were two chaotic fights that happened with the special unit and three unknown individuals. Some onlookers recorded the incidents. Somehow on every camera they were in front of, their whole bodies were blurred," the reporter in a yellow suit and large earrings stated in a high-pitched tone.

Videos were playing back and forth in between her words. Damage to the buildings, street and bus stop location were being shown the most, since it was directly behind her.

"If anyone has any information about the three individuals, please call the NJPD immediately."

"They call themselves the trinity, and until now, they had a 100% kill rate," Radd explained. "So I guess congratulations are in order."

"How do you know this?" Van curiously asked.

"Where is Royce?" Radd realized he needed to ask that first before he continued.

"He left. He was going home to rest, and then we're going back. Oh! there's something you should know. For some reason after the fight, he didn't heal. Van tried to state with the little might he had left.

"Fuck! I figured. Tifini is an energy vamp. If she gets too close and breathes deeply, she can pull out your energy."

"Royce is not going to rest. He needs to heal, but he's not going to, is he?" Van asked Radd.

"Nope, I doubt it."

Van pulled himself up forward. He realized he stayed conscious the entire time. He wanted to put his clothes on. "We have to go."

Radd nodded, and they both discreetly exited.

*****

Night had fallen, and the sky looked more purplish than normal. Royce decided not to go home and head straight to V's tower, ignoring his wounds, which still weren't healing fast enough. He lifted the back seat up and pulled out a machine gun. He slowly looked around before heading toward the entrance. Once he reached the front door, Talan was standing at the bottom of the building when she saw him on a security camera.

"Tifini, Toxis, come here!"

"Tell V first," Toxis suggested.

"Why? We are useless, remember?" Talan said with sarcasm.

They walked out to the side elevator when Royce walked into the lobby, which was empty, holding the gun with both hands as his muscles flexed from the heavy machinery.

He headed toward the elevator and hopped in. Once he arrived on V's floor, he walked through the trees and past the decks and then kicked in a huge mirror-door that fell off the hinges. He saw V and immediately started firing, but the bullets were bouncing off what seemed to be an invisible barrier. V remained with his hands behind his back, standing and smiling. Royce emptied the clip, but there was still no effect. He reloaded and kept the gun pointed.

"Damn, Royce, I really like you! You are the type of soldier I need. That calm rage," V said, still remaining in the same place with his hands behind his back, sporting a small smirk on his face.

Royce offered no response, stepping around the room, shooting three rounds, trying to find a weak spot in the barrier, but with each burst, nothing gives.

"Are you serious, Royce? Stop and listen for once," V said as if he was instructing him as a friend. Royce stopped but kept the gun aimed at V.

"I want you on my team. I'm impressed that you went head-to-head with the trinity and you survived. That's never been done before. They beat you badly, and you still burst into my office like this, and you're all alone. I love it!" V said, clapping.

"I'm done playing games with you. I won't let you reset. I'll die before I let you do this!"

"I like you. You focus on a goal, and you go for it. Even if it costs you your own life," V responded sarcastically. V took a deep sigh and started to look around the room. "You know that's what you're doing, right? You're throwing your life away for something you have no control over."

Royce pulled a grenade from his pocket and then loaded it in the under barrel of the gun and fired. The smoke cleared, but V was still standing there untouched." Royce threw down the gun, frustrated.

"Why don't you drop down your barrier and throw with me then?" Royce threatened.

"Okay," V said with optimism.

Within that second, Royce pushed down on V. V easily blocked each punch even though his punches were causing shock waves, tearing up the room in pieces. The fight began to upfold in what seemed to be lightning speed. V looked surprised, but dodged one to get a clear punch to Royce's stomach, sending out a shock wave of his own. It made Royce yell and drop to his knees, coughing up blood.

"What the fuck? You have my power?" Royce could barely speak.

"No, actually, you are just a weaker version of mine," V said, staring, waiting for the fight to continue when he held out no longer. He punched Royce in the face, causing a shock wave that destroyed the rest of what was left of one side of a wall. It sent Royce flying across the room. V then put out his hand, catching Royce with invisible energy, making him lift off the ground, six feet above.

The sound of thunder was rushing Van and Radd's ears from above when they arrived. They both rushed up the steps to the tower, and Radd yelled out to Van, "They are in V's office on the top of the building?"

"Yes!" Van replied, staring at his holoscreen as quickly as he could to get a visual.

V was still holding Royce up with the invisible force. He intended to end his life but decided to give Royce one last chance.

"Join me!"

Royce tried to speak but was losing consciousness. He tried to concentrate to make a shock wave with his clenched fist, but nothing was happening. He clenched his fist but was still going in and out of consciousness. V flicked his wrist and threw Royce out the window.

Van was still analyzing the screen when he saw Royce's body falling from the sky. "Someone is falling," Van says.

"It's Royce!" Radd said when he immediately looked up.

Radd put both of his hands up, and Royce slowed down as he fell on the truck, only leaving a slight dent.

"How did you do that?" Van asked, shocked.

"Never mind, let's go." They grabbed Royce to put him in the truck to leave quickly.

V reassembled most of his office with his powers, flipping his chair to sit down and make a phone call.

"I need a cleanup here now. There's glass on the front steps."

*****

Radd and Van arrived at his shop and lifted Royce to take him in and lay him down.

"Go get the special unit. It's time they need to know what's going on," Radd instructed.

*****

Standing in front of a podium, Ward was doing a conference. "So we have nothing on the three people in the video surveillance. Royce is missing, and Van has disappeared from the hospital room. Unfortunately, this smells like a hit to me. If we've lost two of ours tonight, we are going to tear this city apart!" Ward said, slamming his fist against the podium.

Van looked around as he walked in, wondering why everyone was standing close to the podium area. Ward immediately saw him, and his eyes widened.

"Where the fuck have you been, and where is Royce?" Ward steadily walked over, glad to see him alive.

"I need the special unit to come with me. We need to hurry," Van insisted.

"Van, what is this about?" Ward did not want to move. "But okay, do I need to bring a normal unit?"

"No, don't bring any normals. It's too dangerous."

"Okay, I'll get everybody ready to head on out. Ward turned around and started giving instructions to the unit, and everyone geared up. Milo and Buster bumped fists and did a man hug.

"It's time, bro."

*****

William walked in at the tower into V's office, stepping on some glass that was on the floor that had broken apart.

"What the hell happened here?" William asked as if was invited in.

"What do you want, William?" V asked, ignoring the question.

"Did you really send the trinity after my son? Didn't I tell you to give me some time?" William asked in a very serious tone.

"You told me?" V stood up from his desk, raising his voice.

"I asked you to give me some time. I saw what happened. The videos are blurred, but it's all over the news. Time would have been less foolish if you would have waited," William suggested in a calm voice.

"The closer I get to the reset, the less I care. I told you to get him out of our way, but you couldn't, so I ended up having to kill him."

"Kill? What are you talking about? He survived the trinity," William asked, confused.

"Yes, that was very impressive, but he couldn't survive me." V put out his arms, indicating all of the damage on the floor and around the building.

William started to look around, realizing what happened. William was speechless. V calmed down. "Let's go for a ride, William."

William didn't want to challenge V and nodded his head yes, hiding his anger.

*****

The night sky fell upon Radd's shop, hinting a purple shimmer, resonating from the orange sky. Everyone was gathered in his basement, surrounding Royce's area, where he lay helpless.

"Is he going to be okay?" Zinda asked.

"The main question is who did this?" Ward interrupted.

"I don't get it, why isn't he healing?" Angelica asked, worried, rushing over Ward's question.

"I'll explain more later. Right now, we need to focus on jump-starting the healing process."

"How do we do that?" Buster asked, interested to help.

"I didn't know he could heal." Milo's ignorance surfaced.

"I should be able to help with that though," Zinda interrupted, knowing she could maximize her powers.

She removed Royce's shirt, putting her hands over his chest. Her hands began to luminate underneath with a purple stream that rapidly started shaking her eyes.

"Okay, Radd, is it?" Ward said, grabbing to pull him aside.

The rest of them gathered around Zinda, waiting to see if they could bring Royce back.

*****

A futuristic BMW with silver chrome curved the corner, gliding across the turn. The wheels turned sideways and back, dependent on the gravitational pull that defies gravity. William was sitting in the passenger, with his long legs barely able to fit. V was in complete silence, enjoying the ride with a cold look upon his face when he suddenly spoke. "I have to fix your incompetence, William. You have failed me over and over. All you had to do was take out the special unit, or at least thin them out. I gave you all the tools to get the job done, the amped vamps and the Grimfurs."

"This is an uncontrollable situation. And you gave the vamp assignment to Cin, so I wasn't aware of everything you were planning," William rebutted.

"Maybe I should do everything myself, because you're not proving your worth, Will," V argued. William stared out of the window, trying to devise a new plan.

*****

Back at Radd's shop, everyone was watching the news. Zinda was still trying to jump-start Royce's healing when he finally popped open his eyes, jumping and grabbing his gun. Zinda was startled and moved back as he dashed across the room, putting his gun to the back of Radd's head, frantically looking around. Everyone looked blurry, and he didn't know where he was.

"Stop!" Van yelled out to come closer.

"Royce! It's us," Ward said to help. Royce finally retracted his gun a bit. Ward took the signal and continued, "He told us everything about the secret war and the reset. Calm down. We're going to help you. We had to jump-start your healing process."

Royce shook his head, still standing there confused, slowing down his movement. Everyone in the room looked concerned.

"Lay down. I need to try to heal you," Zinda encouraged him to calm down when he recognized her voice right away.

Royce, are you okay, what is going on? Van asked to help the situation.

"Now what, kid?" Radd asked since Royce still looked too scared to move.

"What are you?" Royce asked Radd, but Radd stayed silent.

"Oh, nothing to say now? Where's the speeches I love so much, or the advice I had to listen to all this time? I heard everything you told my team, and that was a lot of information that I didn't know you had, so I'm not going to ask you twice." Royce pulled the hammer back on his Rhino 45 while he was holding onto his side, bleeding. Everyone around immediately signaled their hands in the air to stop him.

Angelica intensely stared at Royce, then she looked down at her hands, and they were shaking.

*****

V and William pulled up to Radd's Accessories. They noticed the entire special unit was there. "Radd's Accessories?" William whispered to himself, reading the sign.

"What is this, and why are we here? Wait, is this the same Radd?" William asked V.

"We're here because I'm fixing your fuckups." V indicated that he knew more than he wanted to reveal.

*****

Back in the basement, Milo smelled a scent in the air. "Wait, someone else is here."

Buster followed up after a sniff, "There's two of them."

Ward looked at both of them. "Who is it?"

"One of them is William, the mayor," Buster said as he scrunched his eyebrows, confused.

"I don't recognize the other scent," Milo said.

Outside, V was standing in front of the building, raising both hands, targeting Radd's shop. The building started to shake, and when he slowly lowered his hands, the building collapsed.

"What the hell just happened?" William asked, shocked.

"All of the special unit was in there. See how easy that was?" V told William rhetorically. William stared at the demolished building. Without V seeing, his eyes teared up. He fixed his coat and hopped back in the BMW next to V. The engine ramped up, and the car sped off without them noticing the purple mist started to seep out of the rubble of the building.

*****

The sun rose over a graveyard as the rain was pouring intensely. William was army crawling on the grass. He was beaten and bloody. As he turned over, he saw V standing over him with rain bouncing off his invisible barrier.

"I know what you've been planning, William. I know you really want to stop the reset. And that's why you keep failing me."

William looked up. He stayed silent for a moment, but then he realized he needed to reveal the truth. "The world needs to survive. Everything is a wasteland except for the seven cities left!"

V picked up William by his neck and choked him until he was about to pass out but then threw him down in front of a tombstone.

"I don't understand. We stopped the reset eight years ago. Why are you doing this again?" V had no interest in answering.

"You helped me and Yazmin. Together we beat him and saved the world. You were the second strongest, and you promised to help change the world with us. But now you're changing all of that," William said as he could barely breathe, holding part of his neck with his right hand.

"I lost someone too when we stopped the reset."

V looked up and then William turned around to see Yazmin's headstone. "What is this? What are you saying?" William asked.

"I figured you didn't know. Yasmin was over five hundred years old," V explained.

"What? That's impossible!" William cried out.

"A powerful witch with a power spell. She was mine before you were even a thought. I only keep you alive out of respect for her. But when I reset everything, I can bring her back. She won't remember you, and she won't remember your kids."

"That's why you want to do the reset? You want to bring my wife back?" William angrily asked, making William stand up quickly, barely breathing while holding his neck. He tried to punch V in the face, but his fist bounced off the barrier, pushing him back to the ground.

"You are no longer the mayor. I will announce it tonight. Along with the ending of the special unit. Now I can take over, and nothing can stop me!" V yelled out, which resonated in his villain voice.

V walked away while William lay there, staring at Yazmin's headstone. He wanted to cry, but he couldn't catch his breath.

*****

Zinda was able to move the rubble out of the way, saving everyone from the crushed building, then transporting them to Royce's house. All of the special unit are knocked out on the floor but started to wake up, except for Royce and Radd who are standing in the same position.

"Damn, Zinda!" Ward said, feeling dazed.

"I'm sorry, I've never moved this many people before," she replied.

Once everyone came to, Royce started probing Radd again. "Talk, Radd!"

"Okay, okay! I'm a demon. I used to be a devil, and in V's position, but I was defeated eight years ago."

"What? By whom?" Van asked.

"William, V, and Yazmin," Radd answered

"What the fuck are you talking about?" Royce was pissed and confused.

"I've done three resets. I was the strongest in New Jericho before," Radd explained. "If that's true, then how were you beat?" Buster asked.

"Yazmin, I underestimated her. She's a powerful witch, and while I was fighting William and V, she casted a powerful spell. I didn't know it was even possible, but she gave me a soul."

Angelica looked directly at Radd when he answered and gave a concerned look. "She put a soul in a devil's body?"

"Yes, and when she did it, she killed 80% of my power. Devils and demons are not supposed to have souls, as you all know," Radd said with a sigh.

"Okay, then that is how William and V could overpower you?" Milo interrupted with his question.

"Yes, but at a cost," Radd said.

"My mother," Royce responded.

"Yes," Radd answered.

"A spell that powerful has consequences, and she knew that," Zinda informed everyone.

"She gave her life to save everyone else," Radd praised her.

"And you?" Royce asked.

"This is why I want to stop all resets. The soul your mother blessed me with has changed me completely. I'm nowhere near strong enough to take V anymore, so I'm going to need all of you."

"If we do this, it needs to be done in the shadows. Normals can't know. Most won't be able to process the reset," Ward ordered.

"Yes, I agree. I've seen a world where everyone knew about the reset, and it becomes chaotic." Radd touched Royce's shoulder to answer.

"Didn't you say there's six more cities?" Van asked.

"What?" Buster yelled out unexpectedly.

Milo waved his hands in the air. "This is too much." He crouched over to hold his hand against his forehead, frustrated.

"I need to go to get more ink for Royce," Radd suggested and looked at Zinda as if it was time to go.

"Why me?" she asked.

"Because it's your home city. So it will be our first stop. New Ekron." Royce and Zinda looked at each other, confused.

"Well, I have to deal with William too," Royce claimed. "I'm sure that was V, not your father," Radd answered.

"Well, William was there too, so he's going to also have to pay the consequences for trying to drop a building on our heads," Royce argued.

Ward instructed everybody to rest up. "Zinda, take everyone where they need to go so we aren't seen. Tonight we announce on TV that we are still here because V doesn't know. It's going to be one hell of a surprise."

Zinda created her purple mist to gather everyone, but Royce grabbed Angelica by the back of the neck, pulling her out of the mist before they disappeared. He threw her across the room onto the couch.

"I think we have some steam to blow off?" Royce told her.

"Are you still healing?" Angela asked, concerned. Royce pulled off his shirt and took a deep breath.

"What do you think?" She streaked back to him, and he caught her by the neck, slamming her against the wall with one hand to rip her clothes off with the other.

Angelica smiled. "Well, someone's getting stronger and faster."

Royce smiled, turning her around to pick her up to put himself inside her. Her fangs came out when he put his arm in her face so she could bite down. She became overly aroused and did a kickback to get him on the couch. She jumped on him, biting his neck, regaining intercourse.

"If you bite me, I'm going to rip your head off," Royce warned her with seductive anger as she went down. Her fangs retracted, and he grabbed her hair with both hands to direct.

*****

On the roof of V's tower, purple mist surrounded the edges, and "the heathens" dropped in, beaten, with blood all over, except Denia. She was unharmed, but Ivor's body was cracked.

"I can't believe he was that strong. Next time, you guys need to give me an opening sooner," Denia requested with frustration, wiping blood off of her knives and sword.

"I'm going to need to sleep," Ivor said, looking down at his cracked body. He stepped on to his pedestal and turned back into stone.

Zindo pulled out an amulet from his hoodie and saw it's dull and cracked. "I need to get back to fix and charge my amulet," Zindo told Denia.

"Okay, and I need to get back to the Veil to see if I have any assignments also," she responded.

"Okay, everybody, get some rest. We deserve it, but you all know we are still on call," Cin ordered.

Zindo and Denia disappeared into the purple mist as Cin teleported to William's office. It was dark and empty. Since he was not there, he teleported to the parking garage, but nothing. He landed inside of his vehicle, deciding to take a nap.

*****

At Royce's house, he was getting dressed, and Angelica was still sleeping. He picked up his phone and called Zinda.

"Hey, you busy? Can you come get me? There's a couple of places I'm going to need to go."

A cloud seeped through the phone, wrapping around it, which turned into a bubble inside his living room. She was wearing a blue pantsuit with her hair tied up, wearing glasses.

"Why are you not ready?" Zinda asked him.

Royce walked over to his room as Angelica was lying in bed, still asleep. He quickly started putting on blue jeans and a white hoodie when she saw Angelica through his bedroom doorway.

"Okay, I'm ready."

"Are you crazy, Royce? What the hell are you doing with her?"

"She's a great stress reliever. Let's go. Take me to William's office," he responded, ignoring her concern.

*****

When Zinda and Royce appeared in William's office, he was still not there or in the parking lot. "Where do you think he is?" Zinda asked curiously.

"If I knew, we would be there," Royce said with frustration.

"I thought you said she's a great stress reliever," Zinda said sarcastically.

*****

The night had fallen, and V was starting his press conference in front of city hall. "I called you all here tonight to inform you there will be a new mayor in town, taking over that is. Let me introduce you to her."

Talan walked up in a shiny new black pantsuit with her hair pinned back in a bun. "Her name is Talan."

She shook his hand and posed for pictures. The reporters immediately started to flash their cameras and push their microphones forward to ask questions.

"There will be no questions at this time," V politely directed.

*****

Cin was laying with his head back against the seat when his phone rang. "What do you want? What, are you serious?"

Cin teleported to Philario's office, and Philario pointed to William through the window of the office. Cin looked and saw William at the bar, drinking.

"How long has he been here? Cin asked, staring at William.

"A couple of hours," Philario answered while shaking his head.

Cin teleported to the open seat next to William. "What the hell happened to you, old man?" Cin noticed how beat up William looked.

William turned to him slowly before he sipped his drink. "What happened to me? What happened to you?"

"I was working on my mission with the heathens. But it's all finished now."

"Really? Well, since you're wondering, V did this to me."

"Okay, but why are you in Philario's place?"

"Because I failed." He pointed to the TV behind the bar, watching V talk on the news.

"The special unit is MIA and presumed dead. I repeat, dead. Sad night, but I will return with more news later," the reporter finished her last sentence.

"What the fuck?" Cin was in shock.

"V killed Royce and then he killed all the special unit too," William explained.

Cin's body started to smoke when the news report came back on, and a purple mist filled the screen when Cin and William looked up. The crowd went into an uproar. The special unit appeared with Ward.

"This is great!" V put on a fake smile. "We were so worried about who was going to protect our city."

"We're sorry for the scare, but we all had to go undercover, and we couldn't let you know why," Ward said in an unsuspecting tone.

"That's fine, I'm just glad you guys are all okay." V got in front of the microphone.

"Well, no worries. We can now all get back to work. We will cleanse this city of evil very soon," Ward said to V, staring.

Purple mist started to rise as Royce winked at V, then they disappeared. A commercial came on.

"He's a lot stronger than I thought," William said.

"Yes, well, I did my part. His plan is delayed."

"Are you still sure you can continue on in your condition though?" Cin asked.

William smiled and tapped on his right shoulder with brute force, indicating some of his strength is back.

*****

Trinkets were being thrown across the room by V. He was screaming at the trinity, who were standing on the other side, dodging what they could.

"Are you fucking serious! When!" V finally yelled out.

"We came to tell you as soon as we heard," Talan said with fear in her voice.

"Fuck!" V yelled while stretching the length of his arms out with anger, causing the door and windows to blow out, shattering in slow motion across their faces.

"That doesn't stop your plan, sir. It just postpones them," Tifini stated in a calm voice. V finally calmed down.

"I guess you're right, and he was the weakest. All he had was strength. Do they know who did it, or who's even capable of such a thing?" V asked with curiosity.

"No, they are investigating, but they don't have any leads," Toxis assured him.

"Bring me Cin. I want to talk to him. And Talan, you will be in charge of New Jericho while I'm in New Ekron."

*****

Cin and William were still sitting, contemplating on what just happened when a ring came through on Cin's phone.

"All right, I'm on my way," Cin answered.

"He wants to see me. Do you think he knows?" Cin asked William.

"I'm sure he's heard by now. But just keep your cool."

Cin flashed out of the bar, teleporting to V's office.

V looked up and saw Cin standing there with a straight face. "Is something wrong?" Cin didn't hesitate to ask.

"Yes, I have to leave. But I shouldn't be long. While I'm gone, I need you to do two things," V instructed. "Get the girl from your little gang. Denia, I think it is. And have her follow Royce." Cin nodded his head in agreement.

"Is this to spy on him?" Cin asked.

"Yes, and there is a man named Gemini. He lives in New Hell."

"New Hell? Cin interrupted.

"Yes. In fact, you should fit in well," V said with a smirk.

CHAPTER 11

New Ekron

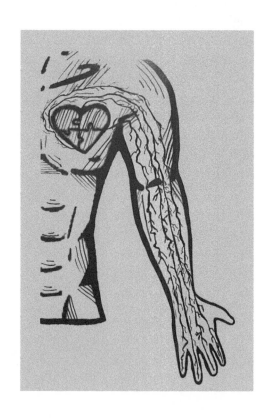

The special unit was standing around in a circular position at Royce's house. Radd was tapping his fingers on the separate chair near Royce.

"Well, Royce and Zinda are going to New Ekron," Ward directed toward the unit. "How long do you guys think you'll be gone?" Ward asked from behind one of the chairs, leaning forward with his fingers crossed.

"If nothing goes wrong, it should only be a day," Royce replied while Zinda stared in his direction.

"Okay, see you when you get back then. And everybody else," Ward said with a sigh, "let's get back to work!" He directed with an affirmative tone.

Van turned over to Royce as everyone gathered themselves to head out. "Royce, I got your car out of the impound for you. We had it towed when we thought you were dead. But it's outside now," Van said with a wink.

"You actually drove it?" Royce asked with scrounged eyebrows. Everyone knew how much he hated to drive if he didn't have to.

Milo was still in the room talking to one of the other guys and overheard. "No, I did," he interrupted.

"Damn, now I gotta clean it. Shit," Royce said sarcastically.

"Well, I could go rip the doors off and turn it inside out to make sure it's clean," Milo responded quickly without even glancing in Royce's direction.

"All right, all right, you win. Let's don't." Royce got up from his seat to end the conversation. Whoever was left in the room started to laugh, but Royce wasn't amused.

Zinda was in the kitchen, sipping on some water, when she walked over to Radd. "Hey, what now?"

"We need to go to Philario's first," Radd answered while taking a deep breath.

*****

Tank was kissing his muscles and talking to some girls outside of the club when he saw them walking up.

"Do you have an appointment?" Tank asked in an annoyed voice.

"Tank, don't do this," Royce warned when Tank immediately noticed Radd.

"Radd, how have you been?" Tank asked.

"Good, you?" Radd answered in a soft tone.

"I'm cool, come on in," Tank turned to a welcoming voice.

"Are you fucking serious?" Royce looked at Tank.

"Well, that is a stress reliever, huh? Zinda tapped Royce on the shoulder as she walked past Royce's frozen, pissed-off face. She immediately giggled as he stayed standing, looking at her with tension.

William was at the bar, watching them walk in.

"Holy shit," William muttered under his breath. "Well, now something makes sense."

William knew who Radd was. He pulled his toothpick out of his mouth and left once they entered Philario's office.

"Well, well, well, long time no see," Philario joked. And, Radd, I thought you were dead," he added.

"Can you help with the halo?" Radd asked.

Philario walked over to a wall, holding his hand up while it read his fingerprints. Once it locked the right blueprint from his fingers, the wall shifted backwards and slid to the left, leaving an opening to an elevator entrance.

"Oh shit." Royce smiled as he followed everyone in.

Tank was left standing behind. "Round two, motherfucker, coming soon," Royce yelled out before the elevator closed. Tank simply smiled back.

They reached a semidark basement. Radd, Royce, and Zinda stepped out, and suddenly, it turned pitch-black, but they took two steps forward, and a large white glowing halo was floating in the center of the room alone.

"What is this?" Zinda asked with deep curiosity.

Radd stared at the halo but then directed his attention to answer her. "This is how people jump from city to city. This is the key to every city in the world. In fact, Royce, your mom made these with other powerful witches that exist in all seven cities."

"Okay, why is it here in Philario's possession? Royce asked with skepticism. "This shouldn't be here." He made it clear that he was upset that it's been in Philario's possession all this time.

"You don't think a shape-shifter that can mimic abilities—not to mention, Royce, he is a small private army with an ogre that has a huge sledgehammer—is capable of guarding it? He's been guarding it for a long time now," Radd tried to explain.

Royce remained upset but decided not to challenge the response.

"Step in, I will do the rest," Radd instructed.

They stepped in and went right through the ring. One second later, a flash of light, they disappeared and then reappeared in a park. The night sky was shiny with a bright-red/pink-like star that was as large as the moon. It seemed to make the trees that had a yellow tint glow in purple with grass that almost looked like green snow. The air was brisk with a sweet smell, and it was very dim everywhere with very few lights to guide them.

"Oh, wow, this is beautiful." Zinda immediately was smitten.

Suddenly, a black peering smoke emerged around them in slow motion that immersed green electricity.

They all took a fighting stance, but Zinda put her hand up. "It's a witch with green power. I've never seen green power before." Zinda watched in amazement while trying to explain.

Zinda powered up, and her eyes started to glow to make her presence known. A purple mist started to cradle the green smoke in a strange design. Royce tried to touch it.

"Wait!" Zinda yelled with a warning.

Royce was automatically electrified by a green electrical current. He screamed and was thrown back to Radd's feet, with green smoke coming off his body. Green glowing eyes appeared in the distance, and it was getting closer through the smoke. Zinda shook her head not to move. A tiny white woman with short red hair, shaved on one side, who is wearing black heels, dark-green pants, and a shirt ripped to show her cleavage stepped out from the smoke with a black duster.

"We don't want any trouble. I've been here many times. I'm Radd. I'm sorry, but I don't know who you are?" Radd turned his plea into a question.

"My name is Minx. I'm the new captain of the NEPD. And if you don't want trouble, you shouldn't have come." She made it very clear.

Minx walked up to the edge of Zinda's mist, waved her hand, and the mist faded away. Zinda's face held a look of shock. "What the…"

"Listen, we just need some ink for my friend here," Radd tried another plea. Royce finally healed and got up quickly.

Minx was surprised. "How did you stand so quickly?" she asked in amazement.

"Sometimes, he's stronger than he looks," Zinda said with a sarcastic cough. Minx laughed and stared at Royce again.

"Well, what should I expect from Yazmin's son?" Minx rhetorically stated.

"How do you know that?" Royce couldn't help but to ask, forgetting she is a witch.

"You radiate energy. You and her are the same, but she is not as weak as you," Minx said with a condescending tone. But something made Minx drop her guard. Her green eyes powered down and turned light blue. Zinda studied her every move from the moment she stepped close and wondered why she would let her guard down. A second later, Zinda looked down and noticed a black cat curling back and forth against Minx's leg. The cat's eyes pierced very green large eyes but appeared to be pleasing to look at.

"I've never seen a green witch before," Zinda spoke out loud.

"We are rare, my dear. But not as rare as Yazmin. She was a white," Minx answered, staring at Royce.

"Did you know my mother well?" Royce asked her.

Minx blinked, and the black smoke faded away. She pointed up into a small distance, and they immediately saw a life-size statue of Yazmin in the middle of the park. Royce slowly walked over. His eyes teared up, and he put his head down as he could not hold one back.

"This is her home city," Minx said, standing behind Royce. "She was my mentor," she continued after Royce wiped his tears off and turned back to her.

"Listen, we need the ink to take down V. We know this is your city, but can you help?" Radd didn't want to waste any more time talking about the past, so he got down to the present.

"V? Victor?" Minx asked and smiled. "Radd, my dear, he is a devil, not a demon. It's going to take more than him to take V down," Minx explained.

"We'll figure it out. But I still need to get stronger," Royce responded.

"Well, maybe if we can figure out who killed our demon, maybe we can help you too," Minx offered a trade.

"Are you serious?" Zinda asked.

"Yes, we found his body a few hours ago," Minx confirmed.

"What? You mean you didn't detect a jump?" Radd was confused.

"They didn't use a halo. It had to be a teleporter or a witch," Minx answered. Radd's lips braced and he sighed. Radd heard Royce, and they locked eyes.

Minx noticed.

"You have information, then?" she asked.

"No. If we find out anything, we will let you know." Radd shook his head.

"Can you help us?" Royce interrupted.

"There is an energy force you will need to fight such a devil, and I know just what it is," Minx said with a smile, showing her pearly white teeth that looked a little scary.

Zinda looked at her with excitement. "So, hey, what about me, you have anything for me?" Zinda asked with a goofy smile.

"Well, for you, we have an extensive library that you can learn from. Suit yourself," Minx answered. Minx clicked her finger, instructing them to follow.

*****

At New Ekron's demon tower, V was standing in the ruins of an office. The top of the tower was completely destroyed. Building security was looking through the rubble.

"Five people were fighting here, and where the fuck were all of you?"

One of the guards acted brave enough to answer, "We rushed here when we noticed the building shaking, but when we got here, no one was here, and everything was already destroyed."

V raised his hand, and all the guards started screaming in deep pain. He slowly made a fist with his hand in the air and started squeezing it as each of the guards started to bubble and blow up into a pool of blood. V stared at the pools of blood at his feet that surrounded him.

"Okay, now are you listening?"

Voices in the pools of blood answered, "Yes, sir, we are."

"Someone killed New Ekron. It was a team of people as we now know, so I need you guys to be on alert. Do I make myself clear?"

Bubbles of blood popped out to answer, "Yes, loud and clear." *BLOOP BLOOP*. V put his hands in his pocket and looked at the sky when one pool of blood asked, "Is the plan still a go?"

V smiled.

"Nothing will stop it. And not to worry. I will stay here another day to investigate who did this," V said in a haunting voice.

*****

Back in New Jericho city, at the NJPD, they were celebrating the return of the special unit.

The music was thumping while the noise from everyone's voices blared over it. The sound of the speakers kept on, but the voices stopped when William walked in.

Van immediately sensed his footsteps and pulled his gun to face William's direction. Behind him, Milo and Buster transformed.

"Everybody relax!" Ward pulled his arms to gesture. "What the hell are you doing here?" Ward sternly asked.

"I came to tell you that I had nothing to do with the building falling on your head," William answered with his hands in his pockets.

"But you were there," Milo contradicted.

"Yes, but that was V. You see what he did to me after that," William proclaimed with a genuine tone. "Also, I need help from Gears," he continued to speak but asked.

Everyone looked around for Gears quickly, confused. Gears was in the back of the department inside Ward's office, eating cake. Frosting slightly covered his nose when he noticed everyone looking at him.

"What?" Gears asked, unaware of the frosting, or William for that matter.

William walked in between the crowd to get to enter the office. The crowd looked around, speaking in secret, but went back to enjoying the music and eating. Van and Ward followed.

"I need Gears to make a gun that kills demons, and I know he can do it." Gears's face drooped as he looked up, knowing that was going to be a hard task.

"Well, do you have the bullet?" Gears asked.

William sighed. "Well, I need you to make that too."

"If a demon-killing gun and bullet were easy to make, everyone would have one," Gears suggested.

"I know, but I have a spell to use on the bullet. I believe Zinda can perform one if she is still strong in her powers," William explained.

"What do I get for this, if it is possible, that is?" Gears asked with sarcasm.

"A demon-free city," William ensured.

"Fucking DEAL!" Ward answered from behind.

Gears rolled his eyes. "FINE, I will start in the morning." Gears picked up his cake and asked Ward and Van to move from the exit door. Van smiled and wiped the frosting off his nose.

"Now you can go," Van said and moved out of the way. Gears smirked and left.

*****

The next morning, in a basement, Minx worked on Royce's tattoo while her cat was wagging his tail, sitting on his lap. She dipped her fingers in the ink, drawing lines on Royce's chest. Her eyes started to glow as she drew the ink that seeped into the skin like magic.

"Damn, cool. I wish you could do that," Royce said as he looked at Radd.

"Whatever, kid," Radd replied.

Zinda was amazed too as she watched on the couch.

"So is there an order to witch power?" she decided to ask, not taking her eyes off of Minx's creation onto Royce's skin.

"Yes, of course. From weakest to strongest, it's red, purple, green, then white. There are only six Whites that we know of. They are all from Ekron and are very powerful. They appointed themselves protectors of the world. And they also authorized one each to be in charge of each existing city.

"I thought there were seven cities?" Zinda asked.

"The one that stayed here with the strongest power became uncontrollable. It killed her. So Yazmin tried to split her time between the two cities," Minx explained.

"So there are seven cities, and six are white. What kind of power did the last one have?" Royce intervened.

Minx looked up but paused and then said, "BLACK."

"Was it an accident that her explosive power opened up the gates of hell?" Radd asked. Minx nodded yes.

"Where are the other white witches? Can't they help us?' Zinda turned to Minx in hopes.

"They are all dead, Zinda. The spell Yazmin used took all of their power. To create a soul out of thin air is a divine power. It took all of their lives at once to do that. And I hope you appreciate that, Radd," Minx directed her answer toward him.

Radd nodded and got out of his chair, feeling restless. He turned about the room to glaze at everything around him. The room was filled with equipment hanging from the walls, some seated on the floor. The carpet was a bright green like the cat's eyes, and the walls were somewhat gray or black but looked transparent.

"So is all this for a training center? And what's behind the vault door?" Radd asked with curiosity.

"Yes, and our halo is behind the vault door," she answered, then turned back to Royce. "You're all done."

Royce put the cat down to stand up, looking in the mirror close by. He saw lines coming from his puzzle heart tattoo going across his chest, down his arm, and splitting into each finger. The cat followed Royce, and Minx watched her cat rub against Royce's legs. She let out a short smile.

Radd turned to Minx as she was fixated on her cat. "So what does this tattoo do exactly?" Radd asked. He broke her concentration.

"It's an energy power, similar to what some demons use," she explained.

"I thought my tattoos were to amplify my abilities. I can't use energy power. Is there a way you can create that?" Royce interrupted.

"We all have life energy. It's just very hard to channel. But it's still life energy, so if you use too much before you heal, you can die."

"So can I shoot the energy from my hands?" Royce replied with a question.

"No, your guns can hold that energy and should be used for that," she answered.

Zinda had gotten lost in the library area of the room. She glared at a book and felt eerie when she touched it. She turned back to Royce, Radd, and Minx.

"Your library is amazing. I found a spell book. Do you mind if I take it?" Zinda asked, fascinated with the book in her hand. It was almost a glowing rainbow that changed colors and flashed in her eyes.

"Sure, make sure you bring it back. But it will ultimately give you a reason to come home," Minx said with another slight smile.

"All right, kids, it's time to go," Radd ordered.

Royce looked at Minx with kindness. "Thank you for everything." He put out his hand, but Minx hugged him instead.

"Anything for Yazmin's son."

The cat was still at Royce's feet. As they walked to the vault to enter the halo, the cat followed. Royce finally noticed. "What is with this cat?"

"Oh, Leo," Minx said as she walked in closer to the cat. "He likes your energy, Royce. He is my familiar."

"What is a familiar?" Zinda looked to Minx to ask over Royce's shoulder.

"It's a spirit or a guide. They protect and assist all witches. Not all find each other, but they can amplify your power. You have a lot to learn, Zinda. You should come home soon and train."

Zinda smiled and nodded in agreement.

They all gathered into the vault as Minx closed the door. A grinding noise started to flare up with some white electric matter, and they vanished from New Ekron.

*****

V was standing near his window, staring out. *New Jericho is a beautiful city*, he thought as he glanced over it from high in the sky. He didn't hear the trinity walk in.

"We are ready to finish our mission," Talan said with a dominating voice.

Toxis tried to complement it with, "We will not fail this time," and Tifini finished their sentence, "And we will kill him."

The doors were closed behind them, but they could hear the elevator open. They looked at each other and saw Denia open the door and begin to walk in. The trinity took a fighting position in a triangle, setting against each other.

"Sorry to just walk in, but no one was at the front desk," Denia said with a smile as her body stood still. "But I suggest you stop aiming for me," she continued.

"You come in here unannounced, so fuck your suggestions," Toxis suggested her own idea in return.

Denia vanished and reappeared at Tifini's face to punch her, sliding her across the floor, then vanished again. Toxis shot a few rounds in her direction, trying to catch her, but Denia appeared behind her with a long curved blade at her neck in one hand and the other blade against her stomach. Toxis was helpless as Talan pulled out her long sword from her side.

V started clapping. "Well DONE, well done. And even though all of this is very impressive, I need to talk to Denia alone. Ladies, you can leave now," V ordered.

Everyone returned to an at ease position, but Talan never took her eyes off of Denia, pointing the sword directly at her face. "This is not over." Talan smiled.

Denia returned a wink.

"So this must be important if the NJ devil himself summons me," Denia told V.

"I need you to keep an eye on someone for me," V requested.

"I'm listening." She calmly sat to listen.

"Royce of the NJPD. He's in the special unit."

"Why am I keeping an eye on this NJPD character?"

"I need reports on his strengths when he fights. I need to know what occurs and if there are any changes in his fighting style or strength."

"*Te veo pronto*. No problem," Denia replied in half Spanish.

V nodded his head for her to leave. "Okay, trinity, back in here," he ordered the trinity, who was standing outside the door. Denia turned to see the door slightly open, and she disappeared to put herself next to Tifini, pushing her to the ground.

"Bitch, I'm going to see you soon," Tifini replied, pulling herself back up. Denia's image didn't appear until she reached the elevator.

"*Muy pronto!*" The elevator shut.

They approached V's desk as V walked out without a word to them.

"I'm tired of this shit!" Talan slammed her hand on the closest desk, and a piece exploded into splinters. "Ever since Royce, we have been put on the back burner for everything. I say we just kill him ourselves."

"Sounds like the perfect plan," Tifini said with a cunning tone.

*****

Royce was standing in the middle of a wasteland outside the city, holding his weapon, Snow. He felt the cool breeze against his jeans and a wifebeater top. Radd stood next to him, watching as if they were waiting on something.

"Man, I'm done. Nothing is happening."

"Let's be patient," Radd counteracted. She said it would not be easy."

Royce sighed, "Let's go see her, it's been two days."

"Let's take a day off and meet back here tomorrow," Radd suggested.

"All right."

Royce drew down his weapon. "All right, Snow, we'll try again tomorrow."

"Hey, where are you staying? I've been meaning to ask you," Royce asked Radd as they walked out of the rubbish.

"Boy, why do you worry about the wrong things?" Radd replied without looking back to walk over to a wall. He placed his hand against it, disappearing into a portal.

"Damn, I need to be able to do that," Royce mumbled. He looked at Snow and pointed to the wall, drawing energy. A small spark emerged, but nothing.

Behind him, a portal reopened.

"What did you forget ol' man?" Royce asked, but when he turned to see, the Trinity was standing behind him.

"GODDAMN IT!" Royce grunted.

*****

Back at NJPD garage, Van and Gears were discussing Van's holoscreen. "Okay, is everything installed now?" Van asked.

"Yup!" Gears replied.

"Thanks, Gears, it's good to have you back."

"Well, someone has to babysit you guys," Gears said in a non-joking tone.

Van smiled and nogged him over the head like the little kid he saw in him. "All right, I'm going to find Royce."

"Tell him I said…" Gears put up his middle finger to finish his sentence. Van smirked and shook his head, walking out.

*****

Back in Ward's office, he was holding a meeting with William.

"Yes, the gun is now complete. I'm about to get with Gears to take a look."

"What about the bullet?" William asked. Ward pulled his desk drawer open with a key. A black little box that jingled came out. He gave it to William to open.

"It's the strongest spell Zinda could put on the object. It's stronger than the original spell you gave us. I also did the calculations. This rooftop address is the cleanest shot if this is going to work," Ward explained.

Ward handed William a piece of paper. He looked at it and then he grabbed it back to put back in his desk.

"Let's go get the gun from Gears," Ward instructed William as he was walking out when he noticed Van standing in the doorway.

"What are you guys up to?" Van asked with his arms crossed.

*****

Royce quickly stayed frozen and faced off with the trinity.

"We still have some business, I see," Royce said with a sigh.

"No, this is personal," Talan replied.

"Your boss must look at you as a failure, considering you couldn't kill me the first time," Royce said sarcastically.

"Your life ends here!" Talan yelled out from behind.

Royce smiled at her. Toxis then pulled out her small handgun that looked like it only fit in the palm of her hand and quickly aimed. Talan pulled her sword simultaneously. Royce rushed the trinity first. He was faster and caught them off guard while quickly punching Talan in the face. A shock wave sent Talan flying back, sliding across the ground. Royce bypassed the attacks from Toxis and Tifini, running past them to catch Talan in her vulnerable position.

"He's gotten faster," Tifini muttered to Toxis.

Toxis quickly turned and shot bullets that flew with a flash of lightning, hitting Royce in the shoulder. Royce slid on his knees, ignoring the pain, to pull his gun from the holster. He returned fire, hitting Toxis's gun out of her hand, ripping her finger off. She let out a loud painful yell.

Talan pulled herself up once she regained her strength. She tried to punch Royce in the back of the head, but he moved to flip her over his shoulder, slamming her on the ground, cracking the cement in half. The rest of trinity rushed him after he punched Talan, sending her back to the ground. Tifini then tackled him down, and she took a deep breath.

"Get the fuck off me!" Royce yelled, kicking her off. She flew back but landed on her feet. Talan, Tifini, and Toxis were now standing in their triangle position, waiting for Royce's next move.

Royce wobbled up quickly.

"Doesn't take much, does it Royce?" Tifini yelled out.

Royce started healing, and he raised Snow up as he had never been hit.

"He's different!" Talan said to warn the girls.

"Very different," Toxis responded with a scared tone.

Toxis ripped off her sleeve and wrapped her hand because blood was dripping everywhere. "Can you still fight?" Tifini asked her without taking her eyes off Royce.

"My other hand is good, but we're going to have to end this fast," she suggested.

"Wait for an opening," Talan ordered.

Talan walked over to pick up her sword and looked at Royce, and he had his gun trained on her. He fired two shots, and she blocked them with her sword. Royce smiled, then put his gun back in the holster. She rushed him, swinging her sword and missing. She backed him to a wall and continued to swing at him, cutting deep into the wall. She tried to stab him straight on. He sidestepped, and her sword went into the wall. Royce kicked the sword, breaking it, immediately followed up by a punch to her stomach, folding her over and taking her head and smashing her face into the wall. Talan fell to her knees. Royce pulled his gun. Tifini ran up behind him.

"Hello again, Royce!"

She took a deep breath and kicked the back of his knee, dropping him to the ground. Talan, still on the ground, took advantage and headbutted him, but it dazed her too. Royce flew backward on his back. As Royce blanked out, Toxis walked over to shoot him in the head. The sky began to glow a bright reddish color. Toxis squinted and looked up.

"Shit! Van is nuking!" she yelled out, withdrawing her gun.

"We have to go!" Tifini yelled, walking over to a wall to open a portal. Toxis and Tifini picked up Talan and carried her through as it closed. Then in a flash of red light, Van was kneeling next to Royce with an assault rifle.

Van cleared the area around Royce. "Damn, are you okay, Royce?" He helped him up.

"Yeah, Tifini is a problem," Royce said out of breath, grunting from the lump on his head. "How did you do that?" Royce asked.

"Gears set me up. I can use the satellite to teleport now."

"Well, you should have got here sooner. I could have used the help."

"Are you okay?" Van felt remorse.

"I'm fine, just a little weak. But round three, all of them will die," Royce said with some vengeance.

"I have an address we need to check out. You up for it?" Van asked with concern.

"Let's do it tomorrow. I need to rest tonight."

"All right. Go home," Van said as he hit his wrist with a flash of light, vanishing.

CHAPTER 12

Gemini

The trinity was standing frozen in V's office, being cursed at.

"If you ever take this shit upon yourselves again, I will personally kill all three of you myself." V slammed his closed fist against his desk, causing a dent in it.

Embarrassed that they failed, they simultaneously answered. "Yes, sir." *BING, BING.*

"Are you expecting someone? No one set an appointment with me," Tifini asked.

"Wait, can you feel that?" Talan asked Tifini.

"That heat!" Toxis answered.

Staring at the door, they heard footsteps when a six-foot Asian man walked in. His hair was long, in a ponytail, and he was wearing a brown suit and shoes, along with a skinny black tube strapped to his back. He was accompanied by a vicious dog, which had scales instead of hair. He stopped to look around, and the girls became frightened, causing them to take a few steps back.

"All right, ladies, that will be all. Leave, and close the door behind you," V instructed. The trinity looked at each other, leaving with caution, still feeling the heat.

"It's good to see you, Gemini," V welcomed.

"V, tell me what you want. I'm not interested in fake pleasantries."

"You will show me respect. What you are doesn't scare me," V responded with anger.

"Is that a fact?" Gemini rhetorically asked. The hound, who is considered a hellhound, dug its claws into the ground with a ravishing growl. V looked down and stepped back.

"That's good, V. You've been gone so long I thought you might've forgotten your powers don't work on a hellhound. Even IF you could kill me, she would definitely rip your throat out."

"Listen, I just want a kill from you. Someone I need dead as soon as possible," V informed with a sigh, sitting back at his desk.

"The mighty V still won't get his hands dirty. Well, if it takes any effort. Who is it?" Gemini demanded.

A detective by the name of Royce. He works in the special unit of NJPD. His trainer is an old man named Radd.

"Radd?" He went silent for a moment. "My usual payment," Gemini seemed to ask.

"Yes, of course." V nodded.

"I wasn't asking," Gemini informed.

V nodded as Gemini gestured to his hound to leave.

*****

The gun had a cutting-edge design that looked like it could take apart an entire building. It was compact with day and night reflex sight.

Ward and William were staring at it, wondering how much damage it could actually do. "It's a long thickly made weapon, isn't it? William noted out loud.

"As long as it's battle ready," Ward complimented it.

"It needs to support the projectile. I'm sure you noticed the bullet is thin as tin metal, but it is as strong as steel. It should be able to cut through anything, and with the power spell, it should be able to cut through a barrier," Gears told them while eating leftover cake from the party.

"It only holds one bullet?" William asked.

"The projectile is designed to fire like a rocket, and it is too thin for a casing. This will produce a small explosion internally that will propel it. So it's useless after one shot," Gears informed.

"What? We only have one shot?" William asked, concern. Ward and Gears shrugged their shoulders.

"Well, one shot, one kill. Good luck." Ward patted William on the back.

William packed the gun, walking out to make a phone call.

"Scout the roof of the address I'm sending you. Then call me back," William instructed.

The address that was given from the calculation of Ward's piece of paper was located close to the center of the city. Van headed over there after nightfall to scope the area. When he reached the roof of the location, he turned on his holoscreen.

Perfect line of sight to V's office, Van thought. He pushed his holoscreen off, and Cin was standing there.

Van quickly swung, but Cin teleported, swapped to his backside to reappear. Van turned to protect himself but is met with a punch in the face. Van fell to the floor but immediately pushed a button on his holoscreen to get an advantage.

"What are you doing here?" Cin asked him, kneeling toward his face. But Van stayed silent. Cin grabbed Van to push him on the edge of the roof, causing him to fall down.

"Damn it, I have to work on the wait time," Van said out loud with a deep sigh.

The roof finally engulfed the red lighting. Cin noticed, looking confused. "What the fuck?"

Cin teleported to the side of Van and threw a punch out. Van disappeared and reappeared next to Cin and kicked him in the face, sending him sliding across the floor. Cin looked at Van, confused. Van took off his jacket and took a fighting stance as Cin stood up.

"I hate technology!" Cin yelled at Van.

"We are NJPD. We adapt to new powers we encounter. This is who we are, what we do," Van said sarcastically.

Cin became angry. He teleported, trying to hit Van again, while Van tried to protect himself from Cin's constant reappearing teleportation that won't seem to stop, but Cin is having trouble landing a solid hit. Van disappeared too, and they were teleporting back and forth, trying to hit each other but missing everything. The red light from the sky started to flicker.

"Shit!" Van yells.

He jumped back, and Cin stopped.

"Well, I'm impressed," Cin said to Van as they faced off.

The light faded, and Van looked down. His battery was low, and the recharge time was thirty minutes. "Well, NJPD. Adapt to this!" Cin yelled out as his body started to smoke.

Cin was just about to snap his fingers when William entered the door on the roof. "What the hell are you two doing?" William asked.

"I thought he was…," Cin started to explain.

"We are on the same side. Go, finish your part!" William demanded.

Cin teleported away, and Van grabbed his jacket to leave. William set up the gun and loaded it. He looked through the scope and could clearly see V's office.

Cin teleported to V's office. William lined up the shot when the door burst open. Royce walked in.

"Damn it, Royce! What the hell are you doing there?" William called out.

William stopped for a minute as he watched. "Fuck it, he'll heal." He continued to line up the shot, but Royce is behind V, and they start to argue.

He pulled the trigger, and the bullet flew with a sharp range of over one thousand miles per minute. It hit the window, going so fast that it made a tiny hole that didn't shatter the window, cutting right through V's barrier. The bullet cut V's ear, and he held his ear with blood dripping through his fingers.

"What the hell was that?" Royce asked.

"Shit!" William yelled out from the rooftop.

V faced the window, determining where the bullet came from. Anger filled his face. His eyes blared as the roof underneath William started to shake.

No way, his power can't reach this far, William thought. He was being pulled through the air toward V's office and crashed through the window.

"I'll let you say goodbye to your kids," V told William as he held him in the air with his power.

"V! WAIT!" Cin yelled, holding out his hand.

"V!" Royce also intervened.

"Finish the mission!" William yelled, barely breathing.

"Time's up!" V squeezed his hands harder as he warned him. William exploded into pieces with blood splattering over the entire office.

"Noooo!" Cin yelled as the room erupted in fire. Cin teleported behind V. His hand in a fist was the first to appear from the teleportation, but V put his hand up and stopped Cin, grabbing his wrist, pulling him forward from the port. A dramatic sound of Velcro was tearing as Cin screamed in pain.

Royce was armed with both his weapons and pulled out Reign from his holster. V immediately launched Cin at Royce, but he caught him.

Royce yelled, "DIE, MOTHAFUCKER!"

Royce's puzzle heart tattoo created a white glow through his shirt. It filtered through the tatted lines coming from the heart, down his arm, and into his fingers. V put his hand up, not knowing what force was coming. Royce shot a clear energy, tearing V's barrier, exploding the entire top of his tower. Cin and Royce were then blown directly out of the building.

*****

At that same time, a man who looked like Gemini but had his hands in his pockets, had stringy oily hair, hunched over, wearing a black hoodie, black jeans, and tennis shoes, with a hellhound walked up to the parking lot at the NJPD. He looked around to see five normals standing around cop cars, laughing and joking.

"I'm looking for Royce," he yelled out.

"There's a shift change, so he could be anywhere. Is there something we can do for you?" the first cop replied.

Wow, what the hell kind of dog is that?" the second cop interrupts.

"It's ugly," the first cop replies.

He grunted at the cops, "The killing kind!"

He pulled his hands out and had long, sharp black nails. He rushed them, slashing the throat of one and punching into the chest of another. The hellhound jumped on another cop who came to help, and started biting his face. The fourth cop started shooting, but it had no effect on the hellhound. He jumped on his back, biting his neck. The last cop was standing frozen with his gun down.

"Who are you and, and w-what do you want?" the cop asks, stuttering.

"I told you, I'm looking for Royce."

The man took the gun from him and put it to the cop's head and pulled the trigger. Zinda appeared and began a purple electric smoke around Gemini and the hellhound.

"Don't move or the smoke will kill you," she claims.

Gemini patted the hellhound on the head and told him to sit. He then started to walk through the smoke. Her eyes glowed, the smoke got thicker, and Gemini slowed as he felt the effects. He dropped to one knee, then jumped out the smoke and landed in front of Zinda, backhanded her, sending her landing on a car. The smoke disappeared, and the hellhound jumped on the car, standing over her, growling.

"Where's Royce?" Gemini asked, coming in closer.

She put up her hands, causing a purple shock wave that threw the hellhound across the parking lot, pushing Gemini back and shattering all the windows in the parking lot. Milo and Buster ran outside when they heard the commotion.

"HELP!" Zinda yelled out.

They transformed, and then Angelica streaked in, hitting Gemini, pushing him back, but caused no damage. Gemini turned to them. "This is going to be fun."

Suddenly, a loud explosion emerged. V's tower was blowing up in the sky.

Ward suddenly also ran out from behind them. "What the fuck is going on?"

The special unit felt and heard a gust of wind and immediately ran out after. They looked where Gemini was standing, but he was gone.

*****

As the tower exploded, Royce and Cin were thrown out of the building in one direction, and V was shot out of another. Royce was unconscious, Cin was trying to teleport, but it was not working. Cin started screaming when he teleported, right before they hit the ground. But V was streaking across the sky, yelling out while he was engulfed in a clear energy from Royce. As the energy dissipated, he fell, going in and out of consciousness. As he put out his hand toward the ground, it opened and shot out fire as he fell into it, then the ground closed.

******

Back at the precinct

"Who was that, and where did he go?" Ward asked with confusion and some anger. Angelica helped Zinda off the car.

"I don't know, but he's looking for Royce," Zinda answered while holding her back.

"Milo, Buster, go to V's tower, and report back as soon as you find or see anything," Ward ordered. They transformed back, then got in a cop car and sped off.

"He killed these normals and did this to you?" Ward asked.

"Yes," Zinda answered, disappointed.

"When I streaked in and hit him, it pushed him, but it didn't seem to cause any damage," Angelica answered.

"Shit! Where's Royce and Van?"

"I don't know," Zinda responded.

Angelica, take her inside, and watch over her while she rests," Ward directed.

"I'm fine. We need to find him. He is dangerous," Zinda recanted.

"I don't want anyone to engage him," Ward said, accepting Zinda's answer. Zinda and Angelica disappeared in mist as Ward returned to the precinct.

"Lock this place down, and dispatch everyone. Let's find Van and Royce now!"

*****

At V's tower, Van was going through the rubble from what's left of the top of the tower when he heard thumps. Milo and Buster came up from the stairs.

135

"What the fuck, Van, you did this?" Buster asked.

"No, I just got here."

"Was V or anyone else in here?" Milo asked.

"I don't know, but there's no bodies here," Buster responded.

"Well, we have to check in," Milo said.

"Don't worry about it, I got it," Van offered.

Van pushed a button on his holoscreen, then disappeared in a flash of red light as Milo and Buster kept looking in the rubble. At that moment, cop cars arrived at V's tower. Gemini was in the suite, not too far on another rooftop, watching.

At the precinct, Van was there looking at the cops guarding the entrances with barricades. He walked in and went to Ward's office and slammed the door.

"What the hell did you do, Ward?" Van asked.

"Excuse me, Detective?" Ward answered with sarcasm.

"You heard me," Van said.

"V's tower. I know you were working on something with William and Cin."

"Cin?" Ward asked, confused.

"Yes, I fought with him at the address you gave William," Van clarified.

"You fought a teleporting fire starter? That's impressive!" Ward proclaimed.

"You're not going to gloss over my question," Van demanded.

"Look, we did have a plan, but there's no way it would've caused that," Ward finally answered.

"Well, the satellite can't find Royce, William, or Cin's biosignature," Van said with concern.

Ward stayed silent.

"Which means they are in another city, dead or dying," Van stated.

"And V?" Ward asked.

"I never had his biosignature?" Van said.

"Shit! Hopefully they're in another city and not dead," Ward responded.

A cop from the bullpen yelled, "Look, turn up the TV!"

Ward and Van ran into the lobby and saw Talan leading a new conference on the breaking news. All of the trinity were bruised and bandaged.

"Yes, we think it was a gas leak. We were closest to it," Talan answered.

"So where's Victor?" the reporter asked.

"He's in a private, secure location," she answered back.

As Ward was watching, he blurted out, "She's lying."

"The last time I saw Royce, he was fighting them," Van said.

"He did that to them?" Ward asked.

"I would assume." Van wasn't sure.

*****

Back at V's ruined tower, Milo and Buster were still looking for clues with some other cops. They felt a gust of wind when they turned around and saw Gemini in a hoodie, standing there with three dead cops at his feet.

"I didn't get to ask you. Where's Royce?" Gemini demanded.

"You son of a bitch!" Buster yelled out.

They transformed and rushed him, swinging and swiping at Gemini, but he easily dodged them. "Last chance!" Gemini rushed back.

Milo jumped over, ignoring his comment, and slashed Gemini across the back. Gemini yelled, and then kicked Buster across the rubble. He then grabbed Milo's wrist, breaking it. He pulled an exotic-looking knife from his hoodie's pocket and stabbed Milo in the side. Milo cried out with a yelp, turning him back to human form, making him fall to his knees, then flat on the ground. Buster was finally able to get up to charge Gemini, but he backed up to the edge of the wall-less room and fell off! Buster jumped off after him and was a distance away from Gemini while he was laughing.

"Stupid mutt!" Gemini yelled out.

In a gust of wind, Gemini disappeared. Buster was stunned and began to yelp as he saw the ground coming closer, but suddenly, purple mist surrounded him, and he was lowered down slowly by Zinda's feet.

"Get Milo! He's hurt bad in the rubble at the top of the tower!" Buster begged.

Zinda made them vanish to Milo's location and grabbed him to bring him back to the infirmary.

"Help me!" Buster yelled out, concerned, as he put Milo on a hospital bed, slipping on Milo's blood. The nurses asked Buster and Zinda to get out. They left for Ward's office.

"What the hell happened? Are you okay?" Ward asked.

"That mothafucker showed up after you left Van! He killed three normals, and Milo was hurt bad," Buster tried to explain, looking exhausted.

"Well, let's go stay with Milo in the infirmary until we can see him," suggested Ward.

*****

Later that night, in a graveyard, Royce and Cin were unconscious near Yazmin's headstone. Cin woke up in pain, looking around.

"Shit, how did we get here?" Cin cried out.

He grabbed Royce and tried to teleport, but he couldn't. Royce was silent, so Cin grabbed him by the arm and tried to teleport again, but nothing. Royce had a gray tint to his skin.

"Damn, Royce!" Cin said with anger that he couldn't teleport. Someone is coming.

"Royce, somebody will help you. This city loves you," Cin said to let him know he was going to leave.

Cin got up and slowly ran off as he was trying to teleport, but he was disappearing and reappearing in the same spot. He yelled in pain, then finally teleported away.

Two drunk men walked up and saw Royce unconscious.

"Holy shit, it's that special unit guy! You know how much street credit I could get for killing him?" the man stated with excitement.

The man pulled a gun, putting it to Royce's head, but Angelica appeared, streaking past him, slicing his throat. The other man turned to run, but when he turned, she was standing there and broke his neck. She stared at Royce for a second, sad at his composure, but she found the strength to pick him up and carried him out of the graveyard as the sun was rising up.

*****

Later that morning at the NJPD infirmary, the doctor gave Ward Milo's injury report. He read it as he walked to his office.

Van was in and out all day, waiting on the report. He asked a nurse who informed him what the report stated, making him run to Ward's office.

"Ward, did you see the report?" Van blurted out.

"Yes, but we need to focus, Van. We need to help Royce, Cin, and William."

"We have a suspect now, a face, a description!" Van said.

"I know, Van, but I think we are being picked off. And we don't even know what he is."

"I know what he is, he's a murderer. It's the same knife, Ward!"

"Van, please, I know he killed your—"

"Yes, my partner. MY BROTHER!" Van slammed his fist on the desk.

Ward knew it hit home and stayed silent to let Van calm down as he looked down at the floor.

"Don't do this, Van, we need you."

"You're reading me right now? Good. I won't have to waste my breath." Van took out his badge and dropped it on the floor.

"Van, look what he's done. You can't do it alone. And I'll say it again, we don't know what he is."

"I'll show him what I can do alone," Van said as he walked out.

*****

At city hall, in the mayor's office, the trinity was having a meeting with a group of people. Talan's eye's swung quickly toward the door when she saw Angelica walking in, interrupting, with the secretary chasing behind her.

"I'm sorry, Miss Talan, she wouldn't stop."

Tifini's eyes grew bigger. "This is impossible," she said under her breath. Talan finally diffused her hidden anger. "It's fine." She cleared throat.

"Everyone, let's finish the meeting later," Talan suggested. Everyone began to leave, and the secretary closed the door.

"How are you here in the daytime?" Tifini asked Angelica.

"I've been upgraded," Angelica made clear while showing her fangs.

"Why are you here?" Toxis made her frustrated voice appear.

"I need to speak with V."

The trinity all stepped forward. "I don't think so," Talan made clear.

"Oh, he will want to hear this," Angelica rebutted, not fazed by the threatening move.

"You have nothing," Toxis replied.

"It's about Royce," Angelica confirmed.

Talan picked up the phone. "Detective Angelica is here with info about Royce. Yes, sir," she promptly said and then hung up. "Come with us," Talan ordered.

They used Tifini's portal to arrive in the lobby of V's tower, got in the elevator, and went down. The door opened, and they stepped into a beautiful gold office made out of glass, with bookshelves from the floor to the ceiling on the side walls. The back glass wall looked out onto the ocean.

"Wow, how is this possible?" Angelica looked stunned.

"Focus on our business." V turned to look at the ocean, brushing her off as a nuisance.

"I want Royce."

"Someone's on it," V confirmed with sarcasm.

"Yes, the psychopath running around killing everyone. If I can find Royce, let me have him. Call off your monster," Angelica pleaded.

"So question first, how are you walking around in daylight?" V asked.

"Focus on our business," Angelica pushed her answer.

V smiled, walked to the window, and looked at the water, then turned and looked at her. "You've been drinking his blood, that's why daylight doesn't bother you anymore," V recanted.

Angelica looked at V, confused. "Your nose is bleeding," she said with a careless look.

V turned and looked at his reflection in the glass, wiped his nose. "If you can find Royce, if he's even alive before 'my monster' kills him, you can drain him."

Angelica knew this conversation was going nowhere, so she nodded her head. When the elevator and the door closed, V sat at his glass desk. Then the entire room changed to a fiery cave as V sat naked in a throne with his whole body bruised and cut. Zindo slowly appeared behind him.

"Good job, Zindo," Tifini said in a nonemotional tone.

"But not good enough. She saw me bleed," V replied with a grunt.

*****

Royce was waking up but still groggy. He stumbled out of bed. He realized he didn't have any clothes on and looked around the room when he noticed two small holes in his neck. Still confused, he took a deep breath.

Why am I naked? he thought before he yelled out, "Dammit, Angelica."

He didn't realize that Denia, who was invisible, was in the room, and without making an appearance, she spoke out, "*Dios mio.*"

"Who's there?" Royce became angry that he didn't see anyone. He kept looking around but saw no one. He looked harder, and the eyes on his owl tattoo glowed white.

"Show yourself!"

An outline of a person emerged, and he quickly got up to swing at it but missed and stumbled. He was able to gage some of his powers right after to push her into the corner and grabbed her neck, even though the force was still somewhat invisible.

"Let me go!" Denia cried out, grabbing his hands. "Show yourself!"

She punched him in the face, took a knife from her thigh, cut his arm, kicked him on the bed, then jumped out the window to escape. He was stunned that she got away and just lay there looking at the broken window before he allowed himself to get up.

"What the hell was that?" Rubbing out his eyes, he was confused to look around again. Out of nowhere, Angelica streaked by, knocking him down, blacking him out.

*****

In a random alley, Radd was running intensely, beaten and bloody. He looked back and didn't see anybody following, so he stopped to catch his breath. He then felt a gust of wind, encouraging him to continue running, when he got kicked in the back, sliding him across the ground on his face. He turned over and saw Gemini in a suit, standing over him. Radd rolled backward, quickly standing to put his brass knuckles on, which were coated with knives.

"Why the hell are you here?" he asked Gemini with frustration in his voice.

"Don't ask stupid questions, I'm an assassin," Gemini replied.

Gemini pulled a sword from the black tube strapped to his back. Radd rushed to swing, swiping at his facial area, but missed. Gemini swung back, but Radd moved back, putting out his hand to send invisible energy at Gemini, trying to knock him out. The energy merely glazed over his hair, causing no damage.

"Wow, they said you got weak, but damn. If you tell me where Royce is or if he's even alive, I'll make your death quick." Gemini stopped fighting, hoping Radd would realize he was going to lose.

"Quick death, so letting me go isn't an option? Radd asked.

"Well, your name is on the list."

Radd turned to run but saw a hellhound sitting at the end of the alley, watching.

"That's right," Gemini stated with a smile.

Radd rushed Gemini, throwing punches, trying to cut him, but he dodged and blocked with his sword. Radd kicked him in the side of the knee, making Gemini stumble. Radd turned again to run, and Gemini followed. Gemini swiped with the sword, but Radd jumped, pushed off the wall, landed behind Gemini, stabbing him three times in the side. He used this to his advantage and kicked him in the side of the head, making him stumble again, grabbed his shoulder, turning him around to punch him four times. Radd jumped, kneeing him in the face, sending Gemini's head into the wall, cracking it. Radd continued to punch him, sending him to the ground. Radd turned to the hellhound and put up his hand, but before releasing the energy, he heard Gemini clearing his throat. Radd looked surprised and turned to look as Gemini stood up, brushing off his suit.

"I don't know why I'm surprised. You've always been a hell of a fighter."

Gemini put his fingers through the holes in his suit and saw very little blood. Radd looked at the blades on his brass knuckles and saw no blood, and the tips were bent.

"But you just don't have the power to hurt me anymore, let alone beat me."

Gemini picked up his sword, swung overhand, but Radd blocked it with his brass knuckles, which caused them to shatter. Gemini then grabbed him by his shirt, headbutting him so hard it sounded like Radd's skull cracked, making his eyes cross. Gemini immediately front kicked with this advantage, sending him across the alley, hitting the wall.

Gemini threw his sword, going through Radd's stomach, pinning him against the wall. Radd screamed, and Gemini walked over to him.

"How the mighty have fallen. Where's Royce?" he asked again.

Radd spit blood in Gemini's face. Gemini grabbed the sword and started to twist it. Radd grabbed Gemini's gripped hand against the sword as he screamed, but when the pain slowed, he started laughing.

"What's funny?" Gemini squinted to ask.

"He's stronger than you," Radd blurted out with the voice he had left.

Radd continued to laugh, and Gemini decided to finish the last twist, pulling it out as Radd fell to the ground, bleeding out. Gemini walked off with the hellhound.

*****

In a dark room, Royce was unconscious, hanging shirtless from his wrists in chains while blood was being drawn through an IV.

******

Ward, Buster, and Zinda are in Ward's office, standing near his desk. "Wait, this is it?" Buster asked, disappointed.

"Royce is MIA, Milo is badly hurt, our allies William and Cin are also MIA, and, Zinda, have you seen Angelica?"

"No."

"And Van?" Buster asked.

"He quit!"

"Radd?" Buster kept going.

"MIA."

"Shit!" Buster slammed his hand against the desk.

I know you two are tired, I know it's getting bad out there. I know we need help, but it's not coming. We assume everyone else is dead, and with V missing too, its chaos. Unfortunately, he did help keep some balance.

"So many NJPD normals are getting hurt or dying just trying to help us," Zinda tried to join in.

"I know that too. No sign of the mystery man? Ward agreed and asked.

"No, but maybe we should just let Van do it since he left us," Buster answered.

"Van can't beat him alone, he will die too. First we need to work this case and let Van track him," Ward suggested.

Ward handed Buster a file. He looked through the pages. "Only werewolves?" Buster asked.

"Yes, well, werewolves are being ripped apart all over the city. I put extra security out on Milo, but this needs to stop now," Ward answered.

What the hell is going on in this city? Zinda asked with severe frustration, looking away.

"I don't know, but we need to get it under control or we will lose the city. Now go, there's an active crime scene downtown," Ward ordered.

Zinda and Buster arrived at the scene and see a crowd of people, police cars, and a werewolf ripped apart. Buster looked around and saw Van in the crowd, then Van walked off. Buster pushed through the crowd and stopped Van.

"What the hell are you doing, Van?" Buster asked.

"Leaving, now let me go!"

"So you said fuck us and the city for revenge?" Buster asked Van.

"Yes," Van replied.

Buster started to transform, but Zinda stepped between them.

"Stop it, both of you. Everyone is watching." Zinda tried to think of something quick.

They turned and saw the crowd watching and recording on their phones. Buster revered the transformation process and calmed down.

"Van, do you at least know who did this?" Zinda asked.

"Yes," he answered.

Van pointed to three men in the crowd with yellow-and-gold-colored eyes, but they quickly turned to run. Buster transformed and jumped over the crowd to chase. Van put his hands in his pockets and walked away. Zinda watched him and, with disappointment, nodded but pulled her gun and shot one of the men in the back three times from a distance. It slowed him down, but he didn't stop. Buster tackled the man, then he started to transform, growing short gold/yellow hair, long teeth, and claws.

"A jackal!" Buster yelled out as he chased him.

The other two men stopped running, transformed, and charged at Buster. Suddenly they were covered in purple mist and thrown into a parked car. Everyone on the street started screaming and running. Three more jackals ran out the alley and were running at Zinda. She covered them in mist and threw them through a glass bus stop. The first two jackals got up and started running at Buster again. She sent the glass from the bus stop at them, stabbing all of them, but they continued.

Buster clawed the chest of the one he was holding down, and it screamed, then more jackals came from down the street.

"We have to go, now!" Zinda yelled out.

She covered herself and Buster in mist, and they disappeared.

*****

On a random rooftop, a man was waiting, then Van climbed on to the roof from the fire escape.

"Van?" the man yelled out.

"Tell me what you know," Van responded.

"What do I get out of this?"

"I'll get you a get-out-of-jail free card," Van confirmed.

"You can't promise that. You're not even a cop anymore," the man proclaimed.

"Wow, word really travels fast," Van said as he smiled and pulled his gun.

"Do you think that makes me less dangerous?" Van answered with anger in his voice.

"Okay, okay, his name is Gemini, and he was hired by V," the man replied with fear.

"What is he?" Van asked.

"No one seems to know what he is," the man explained, still keeping his distance.

"Where is he?"

"I don't know. I hear he was hired just to kill Royce, but since he's dead, he might be gone." Van walked away to think and then in a flash of red light, he was gone.

*****

146

Buster and Zinda were at the precinct, talking to Ward. "Yes, it's jackals," Buster explained.

"I don't understand why they kept coming when they were running at us," Zinda answered.

"Strong pack mentality. When one is down, they will keep coming until they're dead, or they rescue the one in danger," Buster replied.

"Are you okay?" Ward asked.

"Yes, but they have my scent. They will probably come here soon," Buster said.

"Can we take them?" Zinda suggested.

"Alone, they aren't that strong. That's why they travel in packs," Buster explained.

"So they can easily overwhelm you," Ward said, discouraged.

"So what do we do if they come in a pack bigger than we saw?" Ward then continued to ask.

"They will wipe us out," Buster answered.

"Leave," Ward ordered.

"What?" Buster said, surprised.

"You two leave and take Milo with you," Ward ordered.

"Are you crazy?" Buster and Zinda both argued.

"We'll be fine, but if we get wiped out, you two need to keep going," Ward suggested.

Buster and Zinda decided not to argue any longer, knowing how stubborn Ward was. There was nothing they could do. They both took a deep look at each other, and as Zinda walked out, Buster looked at Ward. "Be careful, Ward."

"Just tell me how to kill them."

"I don't know."

"Shit, just get going, and find a way to kill them as soon as you can."

Ward sat for a minute, thinking after they left, but then heard some commotion outside. He walked out and saw twenty transformed jackals and one in human form. Ward walked through the barricade of cops.

"What can we do for you?" Ward walked up to one.

147

"We are here for the werewolves," the jackal man replied.

"Those werewolves are NJPD special unit officers, and they are not here right now. But I'll give them a message if you have one," Ward said, trying to stay calm.

"No, we want to deliver this message in person."

"Then you will have to wait until they return."

"We know you can't take us, so let us in or this will be a blood-bath," the jackal-man threatened. A silence came across. Ward's phone beeped. He looked at it.

"Well, what's it going to be?" the man probed.

"Do I have your word if we let you through, you will not hurt anyone?" Ward asked.

"You have my word. Just want to see the werewolves," the man proclaimed.

Ward got on his radio. "Everyone out the precinct, now! Except Milo and Buster." Everyone came running out of the front door.

"Wise choice," the man said with a smile.

The man transformed, Ward and the other cops stepped aside, and the jackals ran in. "Everybody run now!" Ward yelled.

The jackals rushed in the precinct. But as everyone else has backed away from the precinct to get out of harm's way, a huge red beam engulfed the entire precinct, setting it on fire, demolishing the entire building. The precinct was in ruins.

"Well, that's one way to kill them," Ward said under his breath when he saw Van on a rooftop, looking at the aftermath. He turned away to look at his holoscreen as he sat and leaned against the wall, closing his eyes. "Where are you, Gemini?" He spoke under his breath.

The next morning, Talan was having a press conference at city hall. "Yes, the NJPD precinct has been destroyed while trying to stop the jackal takeover."

"Was any of the officers hurt?" a reporter yelled out.

"No, but there were twenty-one jackal bodies found in the rubble."

"So what caused the jackal uprising, and what about the other crime going on, and the rumors that most of the special unit is dead?" the reporter rambled on.

"And any update on Victor? another reporter yelled out.

"Victor is recovering nicely. We are still investigating the jackal issue and will continue to work hard to get the city back under control."

"And the special unit?" A reporter noticed she didn't answer.

"No more questions, and thank you for coming," Talan cut off the conference.

In the dark room where Royce was hanging, Angelica walked in, slapping him across the face. "What the fuck!" Royce yelled out as he came to.

"V said I can have you as long as I can keep you out his way."

"Are you serious? The reset will affect you too," Royce asked.

"No, he can choose who he wants to leave out and who he wants it to affect," Angelica stated.

"And you believe him? I thought you were smarter than that," Royce replied.

"Well, you are mine if the reset affects me or not," Angelica confirmed in a disengaging tone. Royce looked around and saw the IV and the chains.

"All this for my blood?" Royce argued.

"Yes, your blood has made me stronger than I've ever been. Sunlight doesn't affect me anymore. I'm the strongest vampire in history," Angelica said with her teeth piercing out.

Royce tried to get loose, but he was too weak, so he decided to probe if he could, "What did you do to me? Why am I not healing?"

"Fun fact, you have your emotions under control, but your heart is working too hard to pump the little blood you have left for you to heal," Angelica educated him.

"Angelica, stop this shit. We are supposed to be helping and protecting this city, not handing it to the devil."

"Fuck this city. Your city has killed and outlawed my kind for years. Your city only keeps me alive just to hunt my own."

"V is just going to offer you the same thing Radd offered your father until it doesn't fit his plan, and look where that got him? he tried to reason with her.

"How dare you bring up my father that you killed!" Angelica hissed and streaked to him, biting his side as he screamed. She then walked over to a freezer in the chamber, retrieving two small IV bags of Royce's blood and started drinking one.

"Well, I have to go. Remember, no biting, and you guys can share this one," Angelica said, talking to a dark part of the wall.

Royce looked confused as she threw the other bag in the air, then four vamps ran out from the shadows, catching it and fighting for it as Angelica walked out. As they were tussling over the bag, Royce noticed his IV was bumped, but no one was there.

"I don't know why you are following me or who you are, but you know I'm good and what I'm trying to do," Royce pleaded with what seemed to be the air when Angelica left.

The four vamps stopped and looked at Royce. They walked over to him, and one slapped him. "What are you talking about?" the first vamp got closer to ask.

"Who are you talking to?" the vamp behind him asked, confused.

"I know you're good too because you haven't killed me, and I'm sure you've had plenty of chances," Royce continued to ramble.

"The loss of blood is driving him crazy," one of the vamps guessed.

"Please help me!" Royce pleaded.

The fourth vamp was behind them, sucking on the IV bag when suddenly his head popped off. The other vamps noticed his body drop to the ground, while the two who were standing on each side of Royce got two knives thrown to their foreheads. The one in front of Royce looked around the room to determine where it was coming from, but it was too late. His head popped off.

Denia appeared, standing there with a bloody sword and no expression on her face. Her long hair waved across the front of her shoulders. She walked over to the vamps with the knives in their foreheads and cut their heads off with her short sword.

"Thank you!" Royce said with little energy. She didn't respond. She walked past Royce to a sink, cleaning her knives and sword while he watched. She put the knives in her holsters on her legs and flung the water off her sword.

Royce was staring in amazement. "Listen, I know this is a bad time, but damn, girl, you look good. She stayed silent and cut him down.

"*Estas bien?*" Denia asked in Spanish.

"What?" Royce realized she didn't understand him.

But then she asked, "Can you walk?"

"Get these chains off me, and I'll give it my best shot."

She started to remove the chains slowly, helped him up, and they shuffled out the door.

In an old run-down building Ward, Zinda, Buster, and other cops were setting up. "I can't believe we are back here again," Buster acknowledged.

"I thought we wouldn't see this place again," Zinda agreed.

"Yeah, but we need a base of operations. So this old precinct will be our new precinct for now," Ward explained.

They heard someone from behind, and Milo walked in, looking around. "Nice shithole you got here."

Buster's face had a sign of relief. He quickly walked over and hugged him. "Easy, I'm a little tender."

Zinda walked over and gently gave him a hug, then Ward shook his hand. The smiles on their faces were huge signs of relief, and they knew it meant they had to get back to business soon.

"How are you feeling?" Ward asked.

"A lot better, thanks to Zinda for helping me heal," he answered, looking over at her.

"My pleasure," she responded with a smile, seeing him alive.

"It's good to have you back, man, even if it's not at full strength." Buster offered a fist pump.

"Good to be back. So the jackals?"

"They backed off for now."

"Oh, that's right. I'm going to New Ekron for help," Zinda interrupted.

"Okay, be careful." Ward nodded in agreement.

Zinda closed her eyes and vanished in a cloud of purple mist. "She can jump cities now?" Milo said, unaware.

"She's been practicing and stretching her magic."

"Well, hopefully she'll find a way to quickly kill those jackals," Buster said, looking concerned.

"What are we doing to catch who did this to me?" Milo asked with urgency.

"Van is trying to track him," Ward responded.

"Alone? He'll be killed!" Milo cried out.

"Well, right now I don't have much control of the situation, and I can't have you and Buster running around the city with this jackal problem."

*****

Zinda appeared in front of the New Ekron precinct. There were many cops on standby outside and noticed the purple smoke, alerting them to draw their guns as she appeared. Minx immediately walked out. "Everyone stand down," she ordered.

Everyone lowered their guns and went back to what they were doing as Zinda walked over to Minx. "Hello, Minx," Zinda said in a welcoming tone.

"So you can jump cities already. That's impressive."

"Yeah, I brought your book back, and I have a question," Zinda explained.

"Okay, let's go over to the library," Minx responded.

Minx and Zinda walked through the library, not saying any words yet. Minx returned the book to its original place.

"I need to know how to kill jackals," Zinda asked once Minx seemed ready to talk.

"Wow, I haven't seen any in a while. I know how to kill them, but I can't help you," Minx instructed.

Zinda stared in silence, not knowing how to respond.

"Well, decapitation works for pretty much anything, but the official answer is gold. So for a big pack of them, melt gold into bullets," Minx decided to answer.

"Who the hell has gold?" Zinda asked.

"I couldn't tell you, and believe me, I've looked. If you know any resourceful people, or a superrich in New Jericho, ask them. You never know what they might have," Minx suggested.

Zinda was walking around looking at the books and decided to pick up one that looked interesting. "What's *The Winchester Gospel?*" Zinda asked as she held it.

"I'm not sure, and the dates on the inside cover don't make sense," Minx answered.

Zinda opened the book cover. "2005? But it's 508."

"Exactly," Minx confirmed.

"It's a lot of them, have you read them?" Zinda asked.

"No, I haven't."

Someone called out to Minx's when Zindo walked in. Zinda's eyes immediately illuminated a purple glow, covering him in purple mist, throwing him out the window. He bounced off a cop car and rolled onto the ground. She again started to illuminate the purple glow, but he put up a barrier on the broken window. Her mist tried to push against it, making the barrier scatter, flooding the parking lot with mist, then controlling it to pull in, wrapping it around his neck. He struggled to get free as he fired up his amulet, which started to glow, throwing her against the side of the building. The mist around his neck disappeared as she fell to the ground. She got up and started arcing with purple electricity, and Zindo did the same.

"You got strong. I had to use my amulet to overpower your magic," Zindo explained.

"YOUR AMULET!" Zinda yelled out with frustration.

Zinda raised both hands, but they became frozen.

"What the hell, I can't move. What did you do?" Zinda asked.

"Nothing, I can't move either," Zindo replied.

Minx appeared between them, pointing at both of them, instructing Zinda, "I don't know what's going on, but I can't have you beating up one of my best detectives."

"Are you serious?" Zinda asked.

"Yes, so how do you know each other?" Minx asked in return.

"She's my little sister," Zindo replied.

Zinda tried to break free, but Minx's eyes glowed green and put Zinda on her knees, making her cry.

"I'm sorry to make you cry, but the more you struggle, the more it hurts," Minx instructed.

"No, he killed our parents for that fucking amulet! Then he disappeared. That's the only reason you're stronger than me, Zindo!" Zinda cried out.

Minx glared at Zindo with anger. While never removing her stare from him, she addressed Zinda, "I'm so sorry, Zinda, but I can't arrest him for something he did in another city."

"Do I get to tell my side?" Zindo looked to Minx for sympathy.

"Shut the fuck up, Zindo!" She then turned to Zinda. "I'm going to let you go, but I can't let you attack him. Are we clear?" Minx instructed.

Zinda nodded her head and powered down. Minx released her, and she disappeared in her purple mist.

Once she was out of sight, Minx walked over to Zindo, forcing him to his knees. He powered down as he screamed in pain.

"We need to talk," Minx ordered.

Zinda appeared back in the library, looking at a white amulet encased in glass. She created a small mist cloud on it that allowed her to reach through to take it as she disappeared to appear in Ward's office at the NJPD precinct.

"Tell Gears to make something that melts gold into bullets," Zinda requested.

"Gold? Where are we going to get gold?" Ward asked, strained.

"Tell Buster and Milo to ask Philario," Zinda suggested and again disappeared.

*****

At a beautiful high-rise in downtown New Jericho, Royce woke up and saw glass walls, expensive furniture with a view of the city.

"What the hell?" Royce blurted out loud to himself. Denia walked in, alerting Royce to sit up.

"Oh, sorry I got blood on your couch," Royce announced his apology.

"Don't worry, it's not mine. This place belonged to a drug dealer I killed a while back," Denia explained.

Royce stared, not knowing what to say.

"Bathroom is down the hall, if you want to get cleaned up," Denia instructed.

"Damn you're pushy," Royce alerted.

Royce decided to jump in as Denia creeped behind him to watch, leaning against the wall. "I have so many questions," Royce stated.

"I'm listening," Denia offered.

"Who are you? Why were you watching me? Did someone hire you? Why did you save me?" Royce rambled.

My name is Denia. I am spying on you for V," Denia stated in her sexy Hispanic accent.

"V?" Royce cried out.

"I was supposed to report your fights and strength levels. Don't worry, that's over. I saved you because you are trying to stop the reset and save as many people as you can," Denia explained.

"How long have you worked for V?" Royce asked.

"I don't. I'm with the Veil and the heathens which is ran by Cin," Denia continued.

"Cin?" Royce yelled out.

"Have you heard from him?" Denia asked with confusion.

"No, but he's my brother. Do you know where he is?" Royce asked anxiously.

"No, he's MIA," Denia answered.

"I'll find him soon. What's the Veil?" Royce probed for more answers.

"A group of assassins for hire, but we only kill who we view as bad."

"I'll tell you everything that's wrong with that statement later. But to be clear, the Veil doesn't kill for everyone who offers you money?" Royce stated.

"No," Denia replied.

"So are you from New Jericho?" Royce changed the subject.

"I'm from New Opis," Denia replied.

Royce searched his memory, but nothing. "Never heard of it."

"It's the most advanced city of the seven. So are you healed up?" she explained but then quickly asked.

"Yes, thank you for the eight-hour nap," Royce said.

"Your gear is on the bed. I went to get it while you were sleeping." She directed him to the bedroom, but when he didn't follow out, she redirected herself back to the bathroom.

"Are you playing around in there?" Denia asked sarcastically.

"You can come closer to check if you like," Royce seductively offered.

Royce finally stepped out of the shower, but she only stared to say, "*Impresionante*."

"What?" Royce quickly responded as a towel was thrown in his face.

"Hurry up," Denia replied.

"So I guess you are with me, then?" he recanted. Denia only smirked and nodded.

"First we have to pick up my baby," Royce ordered.

*****

Buster and Milo pulled up to Philiverse, and it looked deserted, but as they reached to open the door, a jackal burst out, running past them. Milo pulled his gun, quickly shooting it in the back, but it kept running. Milo wanted to chase, but Buster held him back, yelling out, "Milo, stop! Chasing is risky. He might meet up with more before we catch him."

They walked in, noticing the place completely ruined. Normals and jackal bodies were scattered around the bar. Tank was sitting on the floor, covered in blood, and Philario was sitting at the bar, also covered in blood, holding a towel on his shoulder.

"Did you get the one that ran out?" Philario asked, looking ragged.

"No, it got away," Buster answered.

"Useless," Philario muttered.

"What the hell happened here?" Milo asked.

"They busted in looking for werewolves, then started killing my security," Philario explained.

"A pack that size was too much," Tank commented.

"Are you two going to be okay?" Milo asked.

"Yes, but we need an easier way to kill them," Philario suggested.

"That's why we are here, to ask if you have any gold." Buster didn't hesitate.

"Gold? That will kill them?" Philario seemed stunned.

"That's what we've been told," Milo suggested.

Philario nodded his head to indicate it wouldn't be a problem. "Rest for a while, Tank," Philario said as he led Buster and Milo to his upstairs office. They used the elevator to reach the lower levels. The elevator door opened to a small warehouse with a safe on the back wall. Philario opened it, and there were some gold bars and jewelry inside.

"Take everything you need. Just get rid of these assholes," Philario ordered.

"Where did you get this?" Milo asked.

"It's crazy what you can find in the wasteland." Philario winked. They grabbed the gold offering and headed back to the precinct.

When Milo and Buster entered Ward's office, they let him know what Gears needed to do. Ward followed them to Gears' shop and called out to him, "All right, Gears, melt this down into bullets," Ward ordered.

"How long?" Buster asked.

"First batch shouldn't take long, but stop rushing me," Gears warned.

"We need as many as you can make before sundown," Ward ignored and ordered.

Gears threw the gold in the furnace to start melting it all down. Milo and Buster smirked at each other as they walked out with Ward.

*****

157

Van was standing on top of a rooftop, looking down, when he saw Royce's truck speeding down the street.

"What the fuck?" Van muttered out loud as he pulled up his holoscreen, pushing some buttons as a red flash engulfed him when he disappeared. He reappeared in the bed of the truck, smashing the back window and aiming his gun at the back of Royce's head as Royce aimed his gun backward, and Denia turned and pulled her sword, pointing back at Van. Royce slammed on the brakes.

"Van, what the fuck did you do to my baby?" Royce yelled.

"Royce, you're alive?" Van exclaimed with shock.

They both lowered their guns as Royce pushed Denia's sword down.

"What did you do to my baby? I just got her back ten minutes ago," Royce was still crying out. "So you know each other?" Denia asked.

"Yes, he's my partner. So I don't know why he smashed my baby."

"Sorry, everyone thinks you're dead. I thought someone stole your truck. Where the hell have you been, and who is this?" Van pointed to Denia with a sarcastic look on his face.

"It's a long story." Royce doesn't explain.

"Well, I guess we both need to catch up." Van relaxed while speaking.

People from behind continued to honk at Royce due to his sudden stop in the middle of the street. Denia pointed her sword out the window at the closest driver, yelling out, "*Cállate!*"

"Well, I know about the jackals? Well, what I saw on the news anyway."

"The man that killed my brother is in town, and he's looking for you," Van responded.

"Me, why me?" Royce asked.

"An assassin or hit man to kill you," Van answered.

"What's his name?" Denia asked.

"Gemini," Van stated.

Denia's eyes widened, alerting them to her knowledge.

"You know him?" Van asked.

"By reputation only. If he's looking for you, we have a big problem," Denia said in a scary accent.

"Well, if he only wants me, I'm sure V hired him. So where is he?" Royce asked.

"I don't know, either no one knows or no one is talking. We need to draw him out somehow," Van suggested.

Denia turned up the radio to tune in on the announcement. "Mayor Talan press conference is about to begin concerning the werewolf murders."

Royce slammed on the gas to speed off.

*****

At city hall, there was a big crowd of people and reporters listening to Talan while Tifini, Toxis, and Angelica were standing behind her. Royce's truck came to a screeching stop when everyone turned to look at them as they all got out of his truck. People moved out of their way as they walked through the crowd.

Van whispered to Royce, "What the hell is Angelica doing there with them? We thought she was dead too, and how is she in the sun?" Van asked.

"Like I said, long story, and just know she's not with us," Royce warned.

Angelica stared at Royce, surprised, and when they got to the top of the stairs, they all faced off. "Royce, we thought you were dead!" Talan cried out.

"Rumors, I'm just here to let the mayor and the city know we have evidence, proving who has been secretly tearing apart the city and plotting to wipe out the NJPD," Royce announced.

"Is that a fact?" Talan viciously asked.

"Yes, and I'm done playing. Bodies will hit the floor. We will take back our city," Royce threatened.

Royce looked at his phone, then walked off, staring at Angelica, and Denia and Van followed. They got in his truck, speeding off. Reporters went crazy trying to ask questions.

In V's office, defined by hell, he and Gemini in the suit were standing, watching everything on the news. V swallowed hard and looked a little nervous.

"So that's him?" Gemini asked.

"Yes, kill him!"

At the precinct Ward, Milo, and Buster were also watching the news. "Damn, where has he been while the city is going to shit?" Buster asked.

"Good question, and who is the woman with him?" Milo added.

"What's more important is why is Angelica standing with the Trinity?" Ward looked stone-cold when he rhetorically asked.

*****

Royce was hauling ass in his truck when they left the scene. He was thinking silently, urging Denia to finally ask, "Where are we going?"

"I got a message saying come to tent city," Royce stated but kept his eyes on the road.

"From who?" Van interrupted before Denia could ask.

"No clue, so be ready for anything," Royce informed.

They pulled up to Tent City, which is under a bridge in an empty water canal full of homeless people. They walked through, and everyone noticed.

"Royce!" a voice cried out.

They all turned around, and a man walked out the shadow, and they saw Radd. "Radd?" Royce recognized the voice.

"What the hell happened to you? Why are you older?" Van quickly stated, noticing his wounds.

"Gemini happened," Radd explained.

"How?" Van asked with growing anger.

"He fatally wounded me and left me to die. I healed myself, but I'm powerless now, and it's causing me to age," Radd said with a grunting old-man tone.

"Damn!" Royce cried out.

"I have one power to give you," Radd suggested.

"That's going to have to wait," Van said and as he interrupted. They turned to see what Van was looking at. They saw the trinity with Angelica. Toxis tossed two spheres in the air above the bridge, and they sprouted small propellers which hovered.

"Shit," Van said.

Denia turned to the homeless people. Denia said, "Vamos!"

But out of shock, no one moved. Radd made a second attempt. "Everyone run now!"

Both sides faced off under the same bridge while the homeless people ran. Radd mustered up some strength to put on his brass knuckle knives.

"No, Radd, you need to leave. We'll catch up later," Royce yelled. Radd hesitated but then ran.

"This is our last time fighting!" Talan yelled out.

Royce smiled, Denia turned invisible, Toxis and Van pulled their guns, trying to shoot each other. Tifini jumped back, expecting Denia to come after her, when Angelica streaked, charging Royce. He punched her in the face, sending her sliding through the tents. He looked up to see Talan in the air coming down with her sword. Royce sidestepped, allowing her sword to cut into the ground. He used this opening to punch her in the side of the head, causing a shock wave, sending her sliding into more tents.

Tifini took a deep breath and saw Denia fade in and punched her in the face, then kicked her to the ground.

"I see you, bitch!" Tifini yelled out with anger, surprising Denia.

Van walked slowly as his guns were drawn around the pillars that held up the bridge. Toxis stepped out and took a shot, but he dove, shooting back. They both missed. He quickly started grabbing his gear to retrieve a smoke grenade and threw it up in the air, running behind the pillar. He looked around, but she was gone. *Damn, she's fast*, he thought.

*****

Talan and Angelica stood up.

"He's so much stronger now," Talan said. Angelica stayed silent.

Talan rushed Royce while Angelica stayed back. She was swiping at him with her sword, missing everything, but then he finally caught her by the wrist. He punched her in the shoulder, breaking it. As she screamed, he punched her in the mouth, creating a shock wave, breaking her jaw. She lost some of her power noticeably, and he punched her in the stomach, causing another shock wave as she fell to her knees, spitting up blood, then falling flat on the ground.

Angelica and Royce made eye contact when he stomped on Talan's neck, crushing it. The shock wave from the brute force cracked some pillars. Angelica never moved a muscle, looking horrified and streaking away.

Van was striding slowly through the dust Royce's shock wave kicked up, looking for Toxis. He heard a beeping when he looked at the closest pillar and saw a small bomb. His eyes widened, and he ran for cover, diving as it exploded. When the smoke cleared, she walked over and saw him on the ground, covered in debris. He was now bleeding from his head. Once she felt it was clear, she promptly rushed away to look for the other girls.

*****

Tifini stood over Denia. Denia did a cartwheel backward, ground kicking Tifini in the chin, making her stumble back. Denia turned invisible again as Tifini caught her balance.

"Stupid bitch, that won't work on me!" Tifini yelled out.

She took a deep breath, and Denia became partially visible to stab her through the chest with her sword. Tifini coughed up blood and fell over.

"*Que pasa, no puedes respirar?*" Denia talked to Tifini, knowing she couldn't answer.

Denia twisted the sword, then pushed Tifini off with her foot. Toxis ran from around a pillar, spotting the fight. She took aim at Denia and started firing. Royce stepped in, taking the shots for her in his back. Toxis ceased firing, feeling a gun at the back of her head.

"You see a little blood and you think it's over? You're good, but you can't finish," Van blurted out before he killed her with a final shot to the back of her head.

Royce was standing directly in front of Denia while their eyes were locked, whispering.

"So how is your bulletproof now?" Denia sensually asked.

"With the reinforced coat against my strength, it hurts, but it's tolerable," Royce responded with a facial crunch, still holding her.

Denia quickly stood on her toes to kiss him when Van appeared, shaking his head in their direction.

Royce turned to face him, ignoring his comedic disapproval.

"Denia and I need to get cleaned up. But keep looking for Gemini, and call me if you find him," Royce instructed.

Van walked away instead of responding as if nothing was asked.

"Van! Don't fight him alone. You heard what he did to Radd," Royce yelled out but didn't carry on.

Van disappeared in a red flash, still ignoring.

Royce and Denia got in Royce's truck to head back to the penthouse to clean up.

*****

In V's hell office, he slammed his phone down and then threw it against the wall. "Where the hell is everyone? Trinity, Angelica, Zindo, Toxis, where are you?"

He was consumed with frustration. He leaned toward his desk to slam his fist against it when his nose started to bleed. He could feel the moisture running down the intersection from the nasal to the lip and immediately pushed his hand against his face to wipe it down. Once he cleared it up, he sat back down, with his back leaning against the chair.

*****

Van ended up at the precinct, watching everyone fortifying the floors. He walked up to Ward. "Damn, what is going on now?" Van asked with confusion.

"One of Buster's informants said the jackals are going to be attacking tonight," Ward answered but was preoccupied while checking his gear.

They walked up to the roof to see Milo and Buster with some other cops setting up and loading guns on the same side of the ledge.

Van walked over to a box of bullets sitting on a table.

"Are these gold?" Van asked Ward when he turned to face him.

"Zinda got the info from a different city. Where's Royce?" Ward answered but changed the subject.

"He's getting cleaned up," Van answered.

Milo noticed them from a small distance and walked over to them, interrupting the conversation. "It's good to see you, Milo," Van said with a smirk.

"Same here. Is Royce coming?" Milo asked with anticipation.

"He's getting cleaned up."

"Cleaned up from what?" Ward questioned with curiosity.

"We killed the trinity," Van replied with a straight face.

"What? You say that like it's nothing," Milo questioned with a concerned look on his face but tried to refrain from looking confused.

"With the girl that he was with?" Ward asked because he knew about Denia.

"Yes, and we need to kill Angelica on site too. So just be careful. I'm sure you've seen that the sun doesn't bother her anymore," Van warned.

"Yes, we've seen that," Ward confirmed.

At the luxury penthouse, Royce and Denia were in the shower, kissing. He pushed her against the shower wall.

"Damn, I'm not your vamp, *la puta!*" Denia said with fire in her voice.

Royce kissed her, picked her up, and carried her to the bed. As they were on the bed kissing, there was a pounding on the door.

"Are you going to get that?" Denia asked.

"No, this is not our place, so it's not for us," Royce stated, trying not to break the mood.

Denia just stared at Royce. "Damn it!" Royce mumbled with frustration.

"It's okay, we have time," she reassured him.

Royce got up, put his pants on, walked to the door, opened it, and saw Radd. He just walked past Royce and sat on the couch, and Royce dropped his head, took a deep breath, and closed the door.

"Damn, Radd, I'm a little busy," Royce said with a sigh.

"So how are you feeling?"

"Good, but I'd feel great if you left," Royce said, looking at the bedroom door.

"You seem stronger. So all that at V's tower was you?"

Ignoring Royce's comments "Me, Cin, William, and V were in the tower."

"Are you the only one to survive? The trinity said V is healing," Radd asked.

"William is dead, Cin survived, I think. I don't remember too much because I was unconscious, but I'm assuming he's why I'm still alive. And V, I don't know."

"Shit, how did William die?"

"Horribly," Royce said, not knowing how to feel.

"So if you did hurt or kill V, how did you do it?"

"I'm assuming it was the ability from Minx. It felt like it was a huge amount of negative energy. Then I guess I was weak and unconscious, for the whole time everyone thought I was dead."

"So you used Reign?" Radd said, excited.

"I guess."

"Wow, if you did hurt him badly, just imagine if you used positive energy with Snow."

"So that's how it works?" Royce nodded his head.

"Yeah, and I have the ink for your last tattoo."

"And what does this one do?" Royce asked.

"I'm just adding a sword and sledgehammer to the anvil. It will increase your strength."

Radd opened the book bag that was on his back, then Royce sat in a chair and leaned forward. "It won't take too long," Radd stated.

"Good, because I was busy. How did you find me anyway?"

"I'm powerless, not brainless. So the trinity, huh?"

"Talan was nothing this time, barely an inconvenience."

"Yes, you are a lot stronger from when we first met. So what did it feel like releasing that energy?"

"Draining. So tell me about Gemini."

Royce glossed over Radd's question. "He's strong and a good fighter.

"No shit, he did beat you. Do you have anything useful?"

"He's from New Hell, but I remember him being stronger."

"But he still beat you?" Royce debated.

"With all the power I lost, but I shouldn't have been able to touch him," Radd informed.

"So are you dying or just aging?"

"Not sure, I've never had to heal myself before, but now I'm powerless." Radd shrugged.

"So what is he?"

"He's a—" Radd paused as they heard a knock on the door.

"Damn, man! I guess I need a Not Welcome mat at the door," Royce joked.

"It's fine because I'm done," Radd said, ignoring the joke.

"The mat is for you too."

Royce got up and walked to the door. Suddenly, the door blew to pieces as a foot came through it, kicking Royce in the stomach, sending him into the living room TV.

"What the fuck!" Radd yelled.

He turned to look at the door and saw Gemini in the suit, rushing Royce. Gemini kicked Royce in the stomach, sending him sliding into the kitchen. Gemini ran after him, then picked him up by the neck and punched him in the chest, then in the face, threw him into the ceiling, caught him as he fell, and slammed him into the kitchen island. He pulled his sword, and Radd punched Gemini in the back only to hurt his hand, and Gemini didn't react. He turned and pushed Radd, making him fly across the room into a wall fish tank, then turned back to Royce.

"Stronger than me? Yeah right," Gemini said while laughing.

Gemini raised his sword. When he brought it down, it stopped with a metal clang and a woman's scream. Denia turned visible in her underwear, blocking Gemini's sword with hers. One of her arms went limp, but she started swinging her sword with the other, and Gemini was blocking everything. Royce stood up and had cuts on his face, bruising on his chest. Everyone stopped and looked at Royce. Gemini looked surprised.

"Royce, are you okay?" Denia asked.

"How's your arm?" Royce responded with more concern for her.

"When I blocked his sword, it dislocated my shoulder, but I'm okay."

"And you, Radd?"

"I'm okay," Radd replied, out of breath.

"All right, Gemini, come get it!" Royce said with cockiness.

Royce took a fighting stance. Gemini put his sword away and smiled. He rushed Royce, throwing punches, but Royce blocked, then jabbed him in the face, making his head snap back. Royce grabbed Gemini's suit jacket, pulled him down, and kneed him in the face, sending him flying through the glass door onto the balcony and leaving pieces of Gemini's suit jacket in Royce's hands. Gemini stood up with a bloody nose and mouth.

"What's wrong? I'm not even using my power yet," Royce asked with a smile.

Royce dropped the pieces of the jacket, and Gemini rushed him, threw a punch, but Royce caught his fist, bent back his wrist, and punched him in the face four times and, on the fifth time, sends out a shock wave, breaking glass and moving furniture. Denia fell to the floor, and Gemini fell to his knees. Royce let go of Gemini's hand, and he dropped to the floor. Royce kicked him in the face, making him slide across the floor through the broken glass door and off the balcony. Royce walked over to the edge to watch him fall. As he watched him, he looked shocked, then walked back in, picked up Denia, and put her on the couch, then helped up Radd.

"Damn, Royce!" Radd yelled in shock.

"Are you sure you are okay?" Denia asked, ignoring her own injury.

Royce smiled as his puzzle heart tattoo glowed white, and the cuts and bruises healed. Denia and Radd looked shocked.

"Yes, I'm fine. Radd, what is he? I thought he was going to hit the ground, but I swear I saw a flash of wings."

"He's a dragon, he's a lot weaker, and he looks different, but I know he's a dragon," Radd said with confusion.

Royce stared at Radd and then looked at Denia.

"Come on, let's get dressed. We have to get to the precinct," Royce told Denia as he stared at her body when she walked to the bedroom.

The sun went down, and they finally reached the precinct, which was fortified from head to toe. They headed up to the roof to meet Ward and Zinda.

"Good to see you around. We could use the extra power," Ward said.

He's powerless. Just give him a gun. He'll do all right," Royce answered

"You want to introduce us to your friend, Royce?" Zinda asked with sarcasm.

"This is Denia, she's been helping me," Royce answered as short as he could.

A silent moment passed when Van appeared in a flash of red light. "What's up, man? Glad you can make it," Royce said sarcastically.

"I was going to say the same thing to you. Looks like you got all cleaned up." Van noticed his messy appearance.

"No, I'm still a little dirty," Royce contradicted.

"Shut up, Royce," Denia interrupted.

"Is it true you guys killed the trinity?" Buster interrupted the conversation with no remorse.

"Yeah," Van confirmed.

"And Angelica?" Milo jumped in.

"She got away, but we'll find her," Royce explained.

"And kill her," Denia finished his sentence.

"You know you can do better than Royce, right?" Buster looked at Denia with a smile, hoping she'd confirm.

"Maybe, but I don't see anyone here that could," she sarcastically remarked as she hugged on to Royce.

"I like her too," Zinda volunteered her opinion.

Royce stayed silent, knowing that she could take care of herself.

"Hey, I need to go get my arm fixed up," she told Royce.

"You can do it here."

"No, New Jericho doesn't have the technology to heal as quickly. I better get going," she recanted.

"Okay, be careful, and come find me as soon as you get back." Royce grabbed her around the waist and gave her a hard kiss to silently confess he was going to miss her. She gave in for a second but then pulled back to hit a button on the forearm of her suit and disappeared.

The guys were all standing there staring at Royce, wondering how he got the girl. "What?" Royce demanded.

"I like her too," Ward antagonized him.

"I told you," Van said.

"Told him what?" Royce asked.

They all started laughing, and Royce was left with confusion.

Loud stomps started to vibrate from the ground, penetrating the roof.

They all walked to the edge and saw about one hundred jackals with Gemini in a hoodie leading them.

"Gemini!" Van yelled.

"Where?" Royce reacted.

"In the front," Ward confirmed.

"No way! I just whooped his ass, and that's not him."

"What are you talking about, Royce?" Van asked with confusion.

"Royce is right. Gemini almost killed me in an alley, and that's not him," Radd recanted.

"Well, that's the man that tried to kill me," Milo indirectly argued.

"And the guy we fought in the parking lot at the other precinct," Zinda agreed.

"Well, who the hell did I fight, then?" Royce asked with a strained look on his face.

"I don't know, but we can figure it out later. Everyone lock and load," Ward demanded. Every cop on the roof, which equaled about seventy-five, took aim.

"I'm just here for Royce and Radd, since he survived!" Gemini yelled from the ground. Or what seemed to be Gemini anyway.

"You think a new outfit is going to change that outcome?" Royce answered and yelled sarcastically from the roof.

Gemini smiled.

"Fine, let's go for round two!" Royce said with a intensity in his voice, ready to fight again. Royce started to jump off the roof, but within a split second, Van grabbed him by his arm to pull him back.

"I got this," Van said.

"Hell no, this is not a game, Van," Royce argued.

"Listen to Royce!" Radd yelled from behind them.

"Hey, Gemini, you're here for Radd and Royce, but they are under my protection, so you're going to have to fight me first!" Van yelled at Gemini, ignoring the guys.

"Is this a joke! Fine, what's one more body," Gemini said with a giggle in his voice.

"It's going to be one-on-one, and when I win, your army leaves. Do you understand?" Van demanded.

"Whatever you want, just come on down here," Gemini confirmed and instructed. Van started to walk to the door, but Royce grabbed him.

"Van, cut this shit out," Buster and Royce both tried to stop him with their simultaneous words.

"We get it. You got big balls, but that's enough," Buster said thereafter, standing close by. Van then looked angry at all of them.

"I got this, partner." Van yanked his arm back.

"Why do you want to do this?" Zinda also pleaded.

"He killed my brother!" he responded with a harsh, loud tone. They became silent for a moment, taking that comment in.

"Walk him all over this damn parking lot," Royce said, encouraging him to get down there.

Van walked to the door while removing his coat. He walked down the stairs and rolled up his sleeves, then pulled up his holoscreen. He pushed some electronic buttons on the left and right side of the device as he was walking through the precinct. Before getting to the front door, he closed the screen back to his original view.

Van walked up to Gemini, and the jackals backed up to give them room.

Back on the roof, the guys were standing in line, facing downward from the edge to watch with anticipation.

"If he dies, it's on you, Royce," Ward said with frustration in his voice.

"I hope you don't regret letting him go," Radd intervened with a pat on Royce's back. They faced down and went silent to watch.

Van punched Gemini in the face, but he doesn't react.

Gemini yelled sarcastically to Royce as he looked up. "You send a normal to fight me? You can't be serious?"

Gemini immediately turned to punch Van in the stomach. Van yelped and slid on the cement backward. Gemini pushed him to the ground when he tried to stand back up, and he couldn't at first, but he finally managed to throw a four-punch combination into Gemini's face. And as he pushed his body upward from a sharp kick up, he smashed Gemini with a roundhouse kick, almost landing on his cheek, but Gemini caught his foot and pushed him back into the cement. He then grabbed him from his vest and slammed him into the ground again.

Gemini then stopped to humiliate him.

"This is embarrassing," Gemini said indirectly while his arms were out, showing his egotistical victory.

"You killed my brother!" Van yelled as he got up and stepped backward, trying to get away from Gemini.

"You would have to be a little more specific. I killed a lot of people, and if that's what this is about, you're a fool," Gemini responded.

Radd, Ward, and the rest of the guys were getting worried watching from the roof. Royce decided to pull out his gun Snow. Radd saw the tattoo lines on Royce's hands start to glow. He was going to take out Gemini himself, but he wasn't absolutely sure if he should fire just yet.

"If I use this, I'll take out as many as I can, but I won't be able to fight afterwards," Royce told the other guys.

"Shit!" Ward yelled. He looked back down to the ground, indicating for everybody else to do so.

Gemini pulled his knife out when Royce decided to go ahead and take aim. "Well, what are you waiting for?" Ward commanded.

Van's adrenaline came rushing in, and he was able to flip back on to his feet to run.

Gemini laughed. "I remember you now. Your brother was weak just like you." Gemini kept smiling.

Van stopped to turn around and face him from a distance. "Why did you do it?" Van was not reluctant to ask in the middle of barely breathing.

"A contract, of course. He was becoming a threat. Maybe becoming too smart, who knows. In the end, it was all fun and money for me," Gemini answered with no emotion.

"You're supposed to be the powerful Gemini, and you have to kill normals just to get by?" Van tried to insult him, and it worked. He charged and grabbed Van by his shoulders to headbutt him, sending him back on the ground. Van got back up, bleeding from his mouth, nose, and a large cut on his cheek from hitting the ground.

"Let me get this right. You couldn't kill a demon at 20% power, and you couldn't beat Royce. I guess killing normals is all you're good for?" Van was still antagonizing the situation as if he had a death wish.

Gemini seemed emotionless but suddenly tried to swing. Van quickly ducked.

Gemini got more angry, and as he swung, he was hit in the head by a small laser from Van's satellite that made him stumble. Gemini rushed Van, throwing a three-punch combination but missed and got hit with another laser to the head. Then he swiped at Van with his nails and knife. After five misses, he was hit in the head again. Gemini was dazed, but he lunged at Van but was hit with another laser that sent him to the ground. He got up slowly.

"What's wrong? You're starting to look a little woozy?" Van antagonized. Van was walking around him slowly but not attacking him in any way.

"I don't know what's happening," Gemini said, confused and dazed.

"You fought my brother twice, and he had our satellite record your fighting patterns. You're not much of a fighter, you're just strong. You use the same combinations over and over again, but once it's been studied, you can be destroyed."

"Looks like I killed the wrong brother. I am a contract killer, but when I kill you, it will be personal," Gemini returned a sarcastic response.

"Well, it doesn't seem like that's going to happen, not even on your best day." Van started to feel victory creeping up on him through his words but was still considering Gemini's threat.

Van decided to let him die alone and started to walk away but turned back to say, "But just in case…"

Van pulled out his gun and shot Gemini in the side of his head. He watched him slowly go limp on the ground. He then looked at the jackals, but they started to run off without an attempt to fight. They didn't even make eye contact when they started to rapidly vanish.

Van began to walk off, but unexpectedly, Gemini let out a wicked laugh while still on the ground with his last moments of breath. Van looked dumbfounded.

"One day I'll make you beg for your life, just like your brother Vinn." Gemini laughed uncontrollably.

Van pulled up his holoscreen and pushed a button. Everything, including the sky, turned red with a glow, and just before the lights hit the ground, there was a gust of wind. When the beam stopped and the smoke cleared, Van walked to the edge of the small crater from the beam but saw Gemini's body completely vanished.

"Shit!" Van yelled out.

CHAPTER 13

The Devil You Know

The special unit and Radd were in Ward's run-down-looking office that barely had decent chairs to sit on.

"So what's next?" Buster asked.

"Yeah, did we stop the reset?" Milo added.

"To completely stop it, we need to make sure V dies," Radd said.

"Well, if he's alive, he's pulling no punches now. He's out to kill," Zinda noted out loud.

"That's true, a dragon and an army of jackals. This is getting out of hand," Van said.

"What I don't understand is why the Gemini Van fought is not the same Gemini Royce fought?" Zinda wondered.

"I'm not sure about that," Radd replied, just as confused.

"Well, let's try to get some rest and worry about this tomorrow," Ward said.

"I think that's a luxury we don't have," Royce said.

They all looked at what Royce was staring at and saw V on the TV in front of city hall, talking to a big crowd of people. Van ran over to turn up the volume.

"Yes, you heard me right. All my staff is dead! The NJPD killed everyone! They said they would purge our beautiful city of evil, but they are killing innocent people. We need to purge the city of these crooked cops! I promise I will make our city a paradise!" V yelled out.

Van's pad on his arm starts flashing and beeping, "What the hell?" He grabbed it.

"What now, Van?" Ward asked.

"Someone is hacking my satellite!"

"What? Is that even possible?" Ward asked.

"Apparently! They are uploading a file."

Van immediately tried to stop it, but when he dialed the buttons to get a response, nothing was working. He sighed.

"Whatever it is, I can't stop it," Van concluded with frustration.

"It's V! He just won't stop," Buster claimed.

"I don't know, but I know it's done," Van confirmed.

"Can you tell me what it is now?" Ward asked.

"No, but it's downloading now," Van said while pressing and holding two buttons on his gear device.

"What to?" Ward asked.

"Every cell phone in the city," Van answered.

"Are you kidding?" Zinda countered.

They all grabbed their phones in anticipation.

At city hall, V was talking, and everyone's phone rang at the same time. The crowd looked, and V pulled his and saw a video starting. It showed V calling for the death of the special unit and hiring Gemini and the order to spy on Royce. The end credits said, "Starring Victor, brought to you by New Opis, and directed by Denia." The crowd looked at V, and someone in the crowd broke the silence by chanting.

"Purge the evil!" And the whole crowd started chanting.

"PURGE ME! THIS CITY WOULD BE HELL WITHOUT ME! V cried out.

The crowd continued to chant.

Back at the precinct

They all just stared for a moment in silence at their phones but then all made eye contact. "Did I tell you I like her?" Ward stated.

"I think you mentioned it," Royce replied.

They kept watching, and they saw V screaming, "YOU WANT A PURGE, HERE YOU GO!" He cried out loud as he put his hand on the ground, and it opened. Black-eyed demons crawled out and started killing people. Punching through their chest, faces, breaking necks, and biting.

"Nooo!" Royce yelled, almost cracking his phone.

"HOLY SHIT!" Van followed.

"Zinda, take the unit, then come back and get the normals!" Ward ordered. Zinda nodded to the order and vanished.

"Everyone put on any gear you got and load up, NOW!" Ward ordered.

Radd and the special unit appeared in a purple cloud at city hall. They saw buildings crumbling from a ground opening, and people were being slaughtered.

"KILL THEM ALL!" Royce yelled out to the unit, staring at V and his demons. V heard him and locked eyes with Royce.

"YOU HEARD HIM, KILL THEM ALL!" V ordered his crew to direct themselves to the special unit to fight back.

Milo and Buster transformed and started clawing and biting the demons. Zinda started levitating debris from the buildings, knocking off demons' heads. Van was shooting, utilizing his lasers from the satellite to shoot demons through their heads. Radd was running and charging at each one to fight hand-to-hand combat, stabbing demons with his brass knuckle blades.

Royce took his opening and charged in V's direction, shooting demons in the head. Just before he reached V, there was a gust of wind, and Gemini appeared in the suit with Gemini in the hoodie, standing side by side in front of V. Royce stopped dead in his tracks.

"Holy shit!" Royce said slowly under his breath.

"That's right, Royce, it's your time to die!" V yelled out when he knew Royce realized there were two.

Even though it stopped Royce in his tracks, he began to laugh.

"Look at them, bruised and beaten. Both of them together can't whoop me," Royce responded.

Both Geminis ripped off their tattered shirts, and Gemini with the hoodie stepped behind the other, then punched him in the back and started to be absorbed. Royce took a couple steps back as both Geminis started screaming.

"What the fuck?!" Royce looked shocked.

Gemini finished transforming. He is now six foot four with a ponytail, who has strands of hair hanging in his face, reptile eyes, light-green scaled skin with dragon wings. Everyone on the battlefield noticed, and battle stopped around him. The stares were distracting them from their own fight.

"There he is," Radd yelled out, recognizing this version of Gemini.

Gemini smiled when suddenly, a swift breeze came through Royce's face where Gemini was now standing. He reached past Royce's head and grabbed the back of his collar, pulled back with the other, punched him in the face, ripping him out of his coat and sending him sliding and rolling, hitting demons in his path until he hit the rubble from the building across the street. He lay there and yelled, "ZINDA, GET HELP!"

Zinda disappeared in the purple fog as Royce tried to sit up as a few demons charged at him. He then saw Gemini opening his mouth, and fire came out blazing toward him, melting all demons in its path.

"*Shit!*" Royce freaked out.

Van was not far off and looked for Royce when he finally spotted him on his holoscreen and gravitated to his position.

"ROYCE!" Van yelled out, but Royce was engulfed in fire. Radd also saw and yelled out his name, but the fire faded out, and Royce was still sitting there but not burning.

"Am I immune to fire?" Royce asked himself as he looked around, realizing what they all realized.

A voice somewhere nearby that he could hear answered, "No, dummy." When Royce looked next to him, Cin was standing there.

"I'm getting tired of saving you," Cin said with sarcasm.

"I'm not," Royce said with a small smirk.

"That's impressive, your fire protected him from mine," Gemini looked at Cin to proclaim with shock.

Then Zinda appeared with the rest of the NJPD in riot gear, guns, and Denia.

"Oh, backup, that's a good idea. Wish I thought of that," V said not far behind. He then started to offer a semi-smile as he slowly put his hand toward the ground again. Several buildings started to burn as the ground opened up in a deep portal sphere, then suddenly, one hundred more demons climbed out.

"Damn it! Take out as many as you can!" Ward ordered.

Everyone started shooting, then Buster and Milo got tackled by hellhounds, getting bit. The NJPD was starting to get overwhelmed, so Denia turned invisible and started stabbing demons, then stabbed the two hellhounds that were attacking Milo and Buster. Then other cops helped them up as more demons closed in while cops were getting ripped apart.

"Everyone regroup! Ward yelled.

As all of the NJPD came together, still firing at the demons, Milo and Buster were badly hurt from the hellhounds, and Radd was holding his side which was bleeding.

"I'm bleeding out!" Radd signaled to whoever he could.

"Milo is going to lose consciousness soon," the cop yelled out to Ward, trying to grab his attention.

"Fuck those hellhounds," Buster grunted with confidence and anger as Denia handed the knife she used to Van.

"Is this the" Van started to ask.

"Yes, one of your cops found it in the parking lot and gave it to me," she answered.

Royce and Cin joined the group, beaten and a little bloody, and Zinda raised purple mist around them.

They got to you, Cin? Ward asked.

"It's way too many, even for me," Cin replied as he was snapping his fingers, setting demons on fire with his flame.

"Van, can you give us a mega beam?" Ward asked.

"No, it's drained, and it wouldn't be enough to win anyway," Van said.

"Should we retreat so we can make a plan?" Zinda said.

"No, we would just be postponing this fight," Ward suggested.

"And if we leave, more people will die, or it will allow him to continue to reset," Royce added.

The demons surrounded them while Gemini was flying above them. V was standing on the stairs in front of what was left of the city hall building, smiling but sweating as his nose was bleeding. Royce looked up to take aim. His energy rushed through his body, lighting his heart tattoo up in a streaming luminous motion through the tattoo lines into his hand.

"Might as well go out with a bang," Royce said, squinting his eye to focus.

"Royce, wait!" Zinda interrupted.

"She's right, Royce. When you use all of it, it will drain your life force completely," Radd enforced.

"What good is life force if you're dead?" Royce argued.

"No, Radd, not that," Zinda started to explain.

Zinda pulled out the amulet she stole from New Ekron precinct library, covered it in purple mist, but then it turned to a white glow as her eyes did the exact same thing.

"Kill them now!" V screamed from the top stair of the ruined city hall.

V's army rushed in when the shock wave from Zinda and the amulet engulfed the city. It turned all the demons to dust and disintegrated Gemini's wings, and he fell into the opening in the ground. When it hit V, he screamed as the ground shook, falling into an opening. The ground closed.

They all looked at Zinda, and her eyes were still glowing.

She shifted her vision to Cin and Royce with glowing white eyes. "What is your problem?" Cin argued.

Zinda was possessed by Yazmin's voice. "Same ol', Cin, always want to be the tough guy."

"Mom?" Royce said with some shock and teary-eyed voice.

"Yes. My babies look so strong," Yazmin said through Zinda.

Cin and Royce looked surprised as Zinda walked to them and touched their faces. Royce shed a tear, and Cin dropped his head.

"I'm so glad my babies are working together. Now finish what our family started, my beautiful boys," Yazmin's voice faded away.

"I'm sorry, Mom," Cin tried to apologize before she drifted off, but when he looked up, Zinda's eyes were normal again.

"I'm sorry, guys, that was the last of her power in the amulet. I can't get through anymore," Zinda confirmed that she was gone.

"What exactly was that?" Royce asked, wiping his one tear.

"It was her amulet I stole from the New Ekron precinct library, but I didn't know her consciousness was in it," Zinda explained.

"Well, good thing you did!" Ward praised.

"I'm sure V is in hell, but we have to follow him and finish this," Royce proclaimed.

"Yes, Mom's last wish," Cin confirmed.

"Royce, this is the last thing I can give you. Give me your left hand," Radd interrupted their conversation.

"We don't have time for another tattoo, old man," Royce responded with anxiety.

But Radd still put out his hand, and Royce shook it. A sudden sensation came over him. "Damn it's burning!"

Radd released his hand, and he saw a thick black-walled circle cut into eight triangles on his hand.

"What's this?" Royce asked, staring at the mark.

"Your portal tattoo you've been wanting," Radd explained.

"Are you serious? I could've had this the whole time?" Royce sounded confused. Radd could not answer. His energy was out, and he dropped to his knees.

"Zinda, take everyone that needs medical attention to the hospital," Ward ordered, staring at Radd.

"I'm staying here," Radd tried to argue.

Zinda nodded yes to Ward and disappeared with Buster, Milo, and other cops. Royce wanted to try his new tattoo, putting his hand on the ground, but nothing happened.

"Well?" Van questioned.

"My power is so low I was worried that the tattoo wouldn't be enough to get to hell," Radd said.

Cin snapped his fingers, and Royce's hand caught fire, signaling Royce to try again. He nodded at Cin and put his hand on the ground, and the portal opened. Everyone looked at Cin, confused, and he shrugged his shoulders. Denia ran over to Royce before he jumped in to hug him.

"*Regresa a mi.*" Royce smiled and nodded.

"Don't forget to use Snow," Radd instructed him.

"Good luck, man," Van offered his worry.

"Everyone here will stay, just in case," Ward ordered.

Royce and Cin walked through the portal, and it closed. Cin and Royce were standing in front of a huge double door in a cave with torches on the walls.

"What the hell is this?" Cin asked, looking around, feeling unsure.

"Hell, probably," Royce offered a joke.

"Not funny."

"I don't know, I just thought V, and this is where the portal took us."

"Well, walking through these front doors is going to be suicide, so I'll teleport us in." Royce put his hand on Cin's shoulder. They disappeared and reappeared in the same spot.

"Damn, can't teleport in. Front door it is, then," Cin suggested with a smirk. He tried to push open the door, but it wouldn't budge.

"Step aside, kid," Royce offered.

Royce pushed on the door, but it barely moved, and Cin laughed. "Oh, shut up," Royce said as he pushed on the door again. His anvil, sledge, and sword tattoo on his back all started to glow white, lighting areas in the cave. He then slowly pushed open the door.

"Well, that's new," Cin said, looking impressed.

They walked in and saw a devilish hall with two rows of pillars with red flame torches, leading to the steps with a throne at the top and V sitting there. As they walked down the aisle, demons were coming out from behind the pillars. As they reached the base of the stairs, demons aligned the walls of the hall.

"I don't know how you got here, but I'm glad you did. Kill them," V said as he sat on his throne.

V looked around as no demons moved.

"Now!" V yelled out as he looked around at them with fiery eyes.

"My guess is you're not powerful enough for them to respect you anymore," Cin said with confidence.

V got up and stood at the top of the stairs. "And you are? With your little fire tricks? And, Royce, with your hard punches? Don't make me laugh," V started ridiculing them.

Cin became angry and, without a word, put his hands together for a new snapping position. When he pulled them apart, they snapped, and V erupted in a blue flame, screaming. V jumped out of the blue flame to the base of the stairs where Royce was on guard as his tattoos were glowing white in full effect. He punched V as hard as he could, cracking V's barrier and sending a shock wave through out of the halls of hell, cracking the pillars in the room. It threw all the demons against the walls. V flew into the stairs, causing a crater. V then pushed an invisible force at Royce, pushing him halfway across the room as Cin teleported next to Royce to help.

"Looks like we both have surprises," Cin blurted out loud as he was ready to fight. Royce smiled as he looked at his little brother by his side.

"He's weak, and he never really healed from our last fight," Royce confirmed.

"And mom's shock wave," Cin responded.

"Just keep him busy, and I'll finish it," Royce said quickly.

Cin teleported in front of V, did his new snap trick, and surrounded them with blue fire. "It's impressive, but you will need more than that," V yelled out.

Cin started teleporting in circles around V, punching him with unexpected, sudden movements. V put up his hands to try and stop Cin from teleporting.

"You're too weak and slow for that to work again," Cin told him.

Cin continued to teleport in circles, punching V. V kept trying to hit him with his energy, but Cin was too fast.

"Yes, you are faster, but you are still too weak to really hurt me," V tried to distract them with his efforts.

"You might be right," Cin agreed with sarcasm.

Cin appeared in front of V, punching him in the face as hard as he could, making V's head snap back. When he looked forward again, he was looking down the glowing barrel of Royce's gun Snow.

"But what about me?" Royce said, pulling the trigger with a flash of light.

Back outside the ruined city hall, Ward, Van, Zinda, Denia, and other officers were standing around waiting.

"Damn, I should've went with them!" Van said, disappointed in himself.

"We all should've went," Denia confirmed she felt the same way.

"We would just get in the way," Ward said.

"Speak for yourself," Denia argued.

"He cares for you, Denia, so he wouldn't be able to focus on the fight if he worried about you," Zinda said.

"So how would we know if they lose?" Van said.

"Simple, they just won't come back," Radd stated with pain in his voice and struggling to breathe.

"Radd, you have one foot one the grave. Zinda, take him to the hospital, and I don't care what he says," Ward demanded.

"No, WAIT!" Radd cried out.

Radd coughed up blood, and Zinda disappeared with him when a portal opened next to them, and Royce walked out.

"Royce!" Denia yelled out with a sigh of relief as she leaped into his arms. He caught her effortlessly as he held her at eye level and kissed her as her feet dangled off the ground.

"Where's Cin?" Van asked.

"He's fine." Royce sat her down but stayed staring at Denia, touching her face and offering a kiss with both hands.

"What?" Van asked for clarification.

"The devil you know," Royce said, staring at Van.

Now that V had been killed, the throne hall was filled with blue flame torches, and demons were at the base of the stairs, kneeling. More demons from around each city were gathering there to honor their new king as Cin was smiling down at them, sitting on his throne.

ABOUT THE AUTHOR

Bruce Bonds, who goes by the pen name B. B. Allen, was born and raised in Toledo, Ohio, as an only child and moved to Kentucky in 2010, where he lives with his two kids. He works in tool and die but always had a passion for science fiction and supernatural genres; hence, he decided to write his first book with more to come.

Lightning Source UK Ltd.
Milton Keynes UK
UKHW010626141222
413904UK00001B/56